MONTANA MAVERICKS

Welcome to Big Sky Country! Where spirited men and women discover love on the range.

THE ANNIVERSARY GIFT

The mayor of Bronco and his wife have invited the whole town to help celebrate their thirtieth anniversary, but when the pearl necklace the mayor bought his wife goes missing at the party, it sets off a chain of events that brings together some of Bronco's most unexpected couples. Call it coincidence, call it fate—or call it what it is: the power of true love to win over the hardest cowboy hearts!

Wealthy bachelor rancher Ryan Taylor has the best of everything money can buy, but since he's discovered he's a father, none of that seems to matter. He'll do anything for Bella—even marry her mother, Gabrielle, the sales rep he spent a memorable week with more than two years ago. He wants Bella to have his name. If he's honest, he wants Gabby to share his bed. Gabby, however, is looking for the real deal, and she won't settle for anything less...

Dear Reader,

Welcome to Bronco, Montana, and the latest installment of the Montana Mavericks. I'm honored to be a part of this particular story as the series celebrates its thirty-year anniversary! So saddle up for the saga of wealthy playboy Ryan Taylor and single mom Gabrielle Hammond.

Moving is never easy, and since I've moved over twenty-four times, I speak from experience. That said, I definitely connected with Gabby, the heroine in *Maverick's Secret Daughter*, as she's the newbie in small town Bronco. Luckily for her, she's relocated to a community full of characters with big hearts and welcoming spirits. Although anyone who's lived in a small town knows that secrets don't stay hidden for long. And Gabby has a cute-as-pie toddler secret whose meeting with her daddy is long overdue!

I always enjoy visiting with readers online and would love to hear what you think of *Maverick's Secret Daughter,* as well as my other novels. Links to my various social media platforms can be found on my website, catherinemann.com.

Happy reading!

Catherine Mann

MAVERICK'S SECRET DAUGHTER

CATHERINE MANN

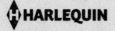

Special thanks and acknowledgment are given to
Catherine Mann for her contribution to
the Montana Mavericks: The Anniversary Gift miniseries.

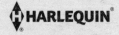

ISBN-13: 978-1-335-59475-4

Maverick's Secret Daughter

Harlequin Enterprises ULC
22 Adelaide St. West, 41st Floor
Toronto, Ontario M5H 4E3, Canada
www.Harlequin.com

Printed in U.S.A.

Recycling programs
for this product may
not exist in your area.

USA TODAY bestselling author **Catherine Mann** has won numerous awards for her novels, including both a prestigious RITA® Award and an RT Reviewers' Choice Best Book Award. After years of moving around the country bringing up four children, Catherine has settled in her home state of South Carolina, where she's active in animal rescue. For more information, visit her website, catherinemann.com.

Books by Catherine Mann

Montana Mavericks: The Anniversary Gift

Maverick's Secret Daughter

Harlequin Special Edition

Top Dog Dude Ranch

Last-Chance Marriage Rescue
The Cowboy's Christmas Retreat
Last Chance on Moonlight Ridge
The Little Matchmaker
The Cowgirl and the Country M.D.
The Lawman's Surprise

Harlequin Desire

Alaskan Oil Barons

The Baby Claim
The Double Deal
The Love Child
The Twin Birthright
The Second Chance

Texas Cattleman's Club: Houston

Hot Holiday Rancher

Visit the Author Profile page
at Harlequin.com for more titles.

To Joanne Rock, my brilliant critique partner,
mega-talented author and treasured friend.

Prologue

Two and a Half Years Ago

Gabrielle Hammond woke up in the honeymoon suite with a hangover, an empty bed and an equally empty ring finger.

Squinting her eyes closed, tightly, she flung the poofy comforter over her head and wished with all her broken heart that she could stay burrowed underneath the downy softness for the rest of the day. The rest of the world was already awake and moving beyond her four walls, a maid vacuuming the corridor, downtown Nashville traffic honking below.

As much as she dreaded facing that world, she had a job to do, a conference to attend.

And she would.

Once she indulged in hitting the snooze alarm a final time while she felt sorry for herself.

Yesterday marked the one-year anniversary since she'd begun dating Bradford and she'd planned a big celebration for his return from his three-month sabbatical overseas. Since she was attending a cattle convention in their hometown of Nashville, she'd decided they could make the most of the five-star riverfront hotel. She'd even upgraded to the honeymoon suite because he'd dropped endless hints about proposing.

Or so she'd thought.

They'd never even made it to the elevator. He'd dumped her. Very publicly. In the hotel dining room, the bottle of champagne she'd purchased sitting in the middle of the table mocking her.

Now, it rested on the bedside table. Empty. But still taunting her for being delusional. She'd loved Bradford, expected to spend the rest of her life with him.

A fresh well of tears burned her already puffy, gritty eyes. Staying under the covers and wallowing in self-pity clearly wasn't working. Time to roll out from under the Egyptian cotton sheets and lose herself in her work managing a booth of veterinary supplies at the convention.

Two pain relievers and a Gatorade later, she handed out flyers, collected business cards and answered questions from ranchers around the world, while videos played on the monitor behind her publicizing the latest products from the veterinary supply company. The massive conference space was packed with tables, booths and convention attendees from around the world. Country music piped through the sound system, barely blanketing the din. Attendee attire ranged from denim to business suits—all sporting Stetsons and boots.

"Thank you for your time," she said to the couple who managed a cattle spread in Texas. "I look forward to hearing from you." Gabby waggled the business card they'd given her, then tucked it into her zipper pouch along with the others she'd received today. While some people darted past her, snatching up the free candy, careful not to make eye contact, she'd also made a solid dozen promising new contacts.

At least some part of her life wasn't a total catastrophe.

She had worked her tail off to put herself through college online, earning a degree in marketing with a minor in animal science, while holding down a full-time waitressing job with extra shifts. She refused to let Bradford's rejection derail her. Her job as a sales rep for a major veterinary supplies company was a perfect fit for her.

Her throat clogged with unshed tears as she looked around the noisy convention center, business booming at the booth next door where a Nashville real estate firm spun a game-show-style wheel to award door prizes. The extra foot traffic had helped generate business for her, too. But the emotion wouldn't let go of her today. She bit her bottom lip. Hard.

"You look like you just lost your best friend."

The deep voice rumbled over her, bringing her back to the present. And what a tall, handsome drink of water that present turned out to be. Mr. Rumbly Voice rested a hip against her demo table. Tall and lean, with blond wavy hair and blue eyes, the man was a doppelgänger for the actor Dan Stevens from *Downton Abbey*—one of her favorite shows to binge with a big bowl of buttered popcorn.

Rather than vintage garb from the early twentieth century, though, he wore typical cowboy gear, the high-end kind from his Stetson to his boots. On the one hand, he fit right in with the others milling about with shiny rodeo belt buckles. But there was also something that set him apart. This guy's charisma added that extra, unquantifiable element that drew eyes. Everything about him shouted rich, confident and determined, no doubt the kind of man women threw themselves at.

Not her, though. She'd had enough of men right now, thank you very much.

And just that fast, her eyes burned and the waterworks started all over again. Sobs bubbled up inside her, the pain right there at the surface pushing past the lump in her throat. Why had Bradford led her on, telling her they had something important to discuss? He had to know what she would think, given the significance of the date.

She snatched fistfuls of tissues from a box by the hand sanitizer just as the cowboy thrust a mono-grammed handkerchief her way.

"Thank you, I'm sorry," she said, mortified, dab-bing her eyes with Kleenex just as he placed the folded cloth on the table in front of her. "That was so un-professional of me. I promise I'm not normally one to cry at work."

"No, ma'am." His magnetic blue gaze searched her, his eyes full of compassion. He shifted his stance subtly, as if to shield her from the eyes of other conference-goers. "I'm the one who's sorry for whatever I said to upset you."

Shaking her head, she finished wiping away her tears and prayed she didn't have raccoon rings of mas-cara under her eyes. "You didn't do anything wrong. It's a long story and it would be even *more* unprofes-sional of me to unload it on you."

"I'm a mighty good listener." He swept off his hat and placed it by a stack of flyers about dietary sup-plements for calves. "Try me."

Any other day, she might have been tempted. "No need to go into all that. It's in the past. So, what can I help you with?"

"I'm fine. This isn't about me." His eyes shone with empathy that called to her.

She pulled a wobbly grin and the sparkle in his

eyes grew brighter. On a regular day, that look would have given her butterflies. But the PA system echoed with updates about the conference, reminding her of her job. So now, she only reached for a brochure to put this conversation back on track. "Let me tell you about our new line of—"

"Where did the cow take its date?"

She blinked in surprise at his interruption. "Um, where?"

"To the moooovies." A dimple dented his cheek.

How could she not laugh? Rolling her eyes, she said, "That was so bad."

He continued, angling closer until his broad shoulders blocked out the live demo on stage, "But it's working. What do you call it when a crazy cow gets loose? Udder destruction."

She snorted on another chuckle.

"That's much better." He nodded, his grin full-on charming and a bit self-satisfied. "What do you call a cow that just had a baby? De-calf-inated."

She couldn't help herself. She burst into laughter, partly from the jokes, but mostly from the corny enthusiasm coming from such a sophisticated fella.

With a final swipe from a fresh tissue, she exhaled, surprised that anyone could lighten the mood on a day like this. But so very grateful for the distraction he'd offered. "Thank you. You saved the day."

"My pleasure, ma'am." He plucked out his wallet and withdrew a white business card. "I've got a whole repertoire of equally witty and corny jokes if you ever find yourself in need. And I hope you do." He held up a hand. "Not that I want you to ever be sad, but because I would welcome the chance to brighten your day again."

If only it were that simple. She took the embossed card and read it, the Triple T cattle ranch logo, home of Taylor Beef, reminding her of work. "So, Mr. Ryan Taylor of Bronco, Montana, do you have any questions that I can help you with today?"

"As a matter of fact, I do have something I would like to run past you." He leaned closer, his spicy aftershave drifting over her. "Will you join me for lunch?"

Stunned silent, she simply blinked. She couldn't have heard him correctly. Was he actually asking her on…a date? He must mean a business meal. "If you will let me know which of our products you're interested in, I can gather materials to show you and arrange a time to meet with you over coffee."

"I already have my latest order heading in today for Taylor Beef." He lifted her hand lightly, his calloused fingers gentle. "I'm asking you to lunch because I want to hear you laugh again."

Flattering. But no.

She began to shrug off his offer. Then she paused. She had to admit, the polished cowboy was good for her very bruised ego. Why not take him up on his request? It was certainly better than eating alone—or worse yet, going up to her solitary honeymoon suite.

It wasn't like she was attached, and her heart was most certainly safe from falling for *any* man right now. Given that Ryan Taylor was from all the way out in Montana, she didn't have to worry about the lunch coming with any expectations or strings or messy emotions. They wouldn't be bumping into each other around town. At the end of the conference, they would both go their separate ways.

And right now, Ryan Taylor looked like the perfect distraction just when she needed it most.

"Sure," she said, rubbing the business card between two fingers, "I would love to."

Chapter One

"Have you contacted Bella's father yet?"

Gabrielle Hammond choked on a bite of her bison burger, the question catching her off guard. She reached for her glass of sparkling water and prayed no one else in the Gemstone Diner had overheard her friend Rylee's question. Luckily, the casual hangout was packed and buzzing with chatter.

Two gulps of water later, Gabby pressed a shushing finger to her lips, thankful her toddler daughter was too young and too engrossed in her french fries to follow the conversation. But there was still a diner full of guests to consider. "Not yet. And I'd like to keep it that way a little longer, just until we're more settled here. The move was a big change for her to process."

She'd thought long and hard before accepting the promotion. The advancement within the company had necessitated relocation from Tennessee to Montana, but the offer had been too lucrative for Gabby to turn down. As a single mom, she needed the money for Bella—the unexpected but cherished result of a weeklong fling with Ryan Taylor two and a half years ago.

Transferring to his hometown a month ago had been bold—and terrifying.

Rylee scrunched her nose as she stirred her straw through her lemon water. "Understood. Still, keep in mind that even though it may seem like the county is spread out, Bronco Valley folks come over here for the employment opportunities offered by some of the…let's just say more well-off people in Bronco Heights, which makes for a tight-knit community. Of course, I will keep your secret but…" Her auburn-haired friend nodded toward Bella, sitting in her booster chair chugging juice from her sippy cup. "Word will get out sooner or later, given how much this little one looks like her you-know-what."

Like her biological father? Yep. Gabby knew she was tempting fate by moving to Bronco, but she also felt like the job offer had been a sign to try, yet again, to persuade Ryan to acknowledge his child.

After their brief affair, when she first missed her

period, she had chalked it up to stress. They'd used protection, after all. By the time she'd realized she was pregnant, she was three months along, terrified and warily excited. Without question, the baby was Ryan's, since she and Bradford hadn't slept together due to his travel before their humiliating breakup.

Gabby twisted her napkin in her lap, the chatter at the next table and the clank of silverware rivaling the roaring in her ears. "It's not like I haven't tried before, Rylee. He totally ghosted me. He ignored my every attempt to contact him."

She'd called the number on Ryan's business card, and got no further than his secretary. Gabby then resorted to the demeaning step of searching for him on social media—only to stumble onto a slew of photos of him with a woman who was obviously his girlfriend.

Still, determined to do the right thing, she had sent him a DM asking him to contact her. Immediately. He'd never replied. The jerk.

Next, she'd sent letters to his work address telling him she needed to talk. It was an emergency. Still, he'd never replied.

That was all the answer she'd needed. She wasn't about to make a fool of herself by chasing him. Gabby had her life on track professionally. She didn't need a man. Her daughter and her mini-Australian shepherd, Elsie, were all the family she needed.

Rylee squeezed her hand. "I'm sorry. I didn't mean

to pry." She'd been told all the details during a late-night gab session with popcorn and wine. "You've trusted me and I appreciate that. I know we're new friends, but I feel as if I've known you my whole life. I guess you could say we're kindred spirits."

"Thank you. I feel absolutely the same." Her friendship with Rylee Parker had been a sanity saver since her arrival in Montana. Gabby squeezed her hand back, then passed Bella more fries off her plate, just barely keeping her daughter from pitching her sippy cup. Again. "I'll find a way to tell him when the time is right." She'd seen him from a distance but hadn't worked up the nerve. "I still haven't even unpacked all my boxes."

Rylee quirked a delicately arched eyebrow. "Okay. I wouldn't dare say that sounds like a stall tactic."

"Fair. I just don't want to deliver the news over the phone." If she could even get through, unlike before. Emails hadn't worked, either. "I can't imagine just showing up at his door unannounced."

"I don't think that would work anyway," Rylee said. Quiet, brainy, a little shy, she had no idea how pretty she was. But she rocked her job as marketing director of the Bronco Convention Center. "Taylor Beef is a business, Gabby. They've got employees—some of whom are family. It's not exactly private. And it's unlikely you could just drive onto the Triple T Ranch property."

"Good point. Maybe I should just make a business

appointment to see him, as if I'm reaching out about veterinary supplies." It felt good to have someone to talk this through with. Since arriving in Bronco a month ago, she was already making amazing new friends, especially Rylee Parker. Rylee had also been a lifesaver in watching Bella on occasion.

"Do you know what you'll say?"

Gabby winced. "There's no easy way to break the news. I guess I'll just get to the point. Rip the bandage off, so to speak."

"That makes sense." Rylee nodded, her blue eyes sweetly understanding. "I'm sorry if my questions are pushy."

Shaking her head, Gabby swept her hair back over her shoulder. "You're anything but pushy. I'm so thankful for you. I don't know how I'll ever repay you for all you've done to help me since I moved here."

"Friendship doesn't come with a price tag. Although thank you for inviting me to lunch."

"Bella adores you, too." Gabby smoothed a hand over her daughter's silky brown hair, adjusting the lopsided bow. "You're good with her."

"I love kids. I always thought that I'd be married with a family of my own by thirty, but since the big three-oh is coming up," she said with a shrug, "it just doesn't seem to be in the cards for me unless something changes soon. My marketing work—and my friends—make for a full life. Someday, maybe…"

Bella chucked her sippy cup on the floor. Her fa-vorite pastime—after coloring on the walls.

"Hold that thought," Gabby said, leaning down to retrieve the pink-flowered plastic cup. Except it had rolled under the table. She slid from her seat, kneel-ing, ducking under the red-checkered tablecloth until her hands closed around the handle.

"Uh, Gabby…" Rylee's wary voice drifted from above.

"Just a minute. I've almost got it." She loved her precious baby girl, but this game was getting old and everything she'd read about childhood development indicated this stage of asserting toddler impishness—a.k.a. independence—was far from over.

"Psst, Gabby," Rylee said again, more insistently.

Gabby inched backward, awkwardly, trying not to dirty her knees, all too aware of her snug slacks. Protecting her dignity slowed her progress, but there hadn't been time to change from her work clothes—a pantsuit and pressed cotton button-down with her business logo. Her knees were probably covered in mushed fries and the fabric was no doubt stretched to the limit around her butt.

Finally, she stood, returning the cup to Bella's tray and smoothing her slacks back into place. Although, no doubt, her daughter would toss the cup again—and again. "Okay, Rylee. What's up?"

Her friend's blue eyes were full of something that

looked a lot like panic. And what was that she was doing with her hand? Why was she twitching her head?

Then Rylee pointed with deliberation. "Look. Behind. You."

A deep sense of foreboding washed over Gabby as she pivoted on her black leather pumps. And her gaze landed on *him*. Her stomach dropped as if she were on the scariest roller-coaster ride plunging to earth.

Fate wasn't done with her yet. The tight-knit town of Bronco, Montana, had gotten a lot smaller.

Because Ryan Taylor had just walked through the door.

Ryan Taylor hoped his order was ready and waiting because he didn't have one more minute to spare in an already packed Saturday work schedule where he hadn't been able to break for anything other than a carryout lunch. He missed the simpler days when he was free to ride the ranch with his five siblings, days spent on a cattle drive or breaking in a wild mustang.

Lately, he spent more time in an office and in suits than in the saddle and boots. But such was his life with Taylor Beef, a family legacy to be protected. Just ask his dad. But the land, the Triple T—Ryan's first and deepest love—was tied to the family business. If he wanted to keep that love, he had to make his mark in Taylor Beef.

So meals on the go were a must, more often than not, and tonight would be a late one in the office.

At least the line to the carryout counter wasn't long, even though every table was occupied. The echo of chatter and clinking silverware swelled from dining-in customers. The food was top-notch, made with farm-fresh ingredients, worth far more than the reasonable price. With a smile and a generous tip, he snagged the container for himself and a second for his personal assistant. His stomach grumbled for the venison barbecue sandwich, slaw and a slice of huckleberry pie in his order.

Pivoting, he made fast tracks toward the exit, weaving around tables and waitstaff. Only to stop short. The hairs on the back of his neck stood on alert, just before a hint of honeysuckle stirred his memory. Every time he'd caught a whiff of that scent over the past two years, he thought of the unforgettable fling with Gabrielle Hammond. Except she was in Nashville. They'd agreed the encounter was short term. He'd moved on with his girlfriend, Nora, an uncomplicated on-again, off-again relationship.

Currently in an off stage.

He knew the past with Gabby was the past, no more than a fond memory. Still, he couldn't stop himself from hesitating, just for a moment, tipping his head toward the flowery scent to find...

What? It couldn't be. Not here, after all this time. Surely the shapely woman with thick brown hair was just a look-alike version of Gabrielle Hammond.

Or a figment of his imagination and, yes, midnight fantasies.

Yet, as he blinked, the vision of her remained the same.

Everything from the curves to her gently beautiful face was familiar. And yes, he remembered well those brown eyes with long lashes, so full of life and fun. Her allure wasn't the product of perfectly applied makeup or flashy clothes. Her appeal was all-natural. And he was totally drawn in. Now just as he'd been years ago.

He secured his hold on his cardboard containers and moved closer. From the way she stared back at him, her eyes wide with surprise, she recognized him, as well. As he drew nearer, he saw more than surprise, more like panic. Why? The level of emotion seemed over the top. Sure, they'd shared a passionate week, a connection, but it had been a fling. Nothing more. Right?

Stopping by the corner table, he briefly noted her dining companion, a redheaded woman scooping up a sippy cup and passing it to the cute little toddler stuffing fries into her face.

He pulled his attention away from the mother and daughter and back to… "Gabrielle?"

She pulled a tight smile. "Hello, Ryan."

So she recognized him. How embarrassing it would have been if she hadn't. "What brings you to Bronco?"

"My job. I was offered a transfer, working on rodeo business. I only moved here a month ago," she said quickly, shifting from foot to foot, looking agitated. "Have you met my new friend Rylee Parker? And this is, uh, Bella."

She stared at him so hard, he wondered if he had something between his teeth.

"Cute kid." He nodded to Rylee before returning his attention to Gabrielle—Gabby, she'd told him she preferred to be called. She'd said the words over a room service meal, plucking a fry off his plate playfully.

He swallowed back the memory. Sure, he'd dreamed about her more than once, but he didn't have time to deep-dive into the past right now. He needed to get back to work. He'd poured his lifeblood into Taylor Beef.

Gabby fished in her purse, then pulled out a business card. "Um, here's my info, updated since I relocated last month."

Was she still attracted, too? Or was it just a professional courtesy? She wasn't wearing a wedding ring.

Something to mull over later. For now, he had to get back to the office fast and eat before his next meeting.

He set down his cardboard containers on her table and pocketed the card. "Well, I won't disrupt your lunch, ladies." He retrieved his food. "It was nice to meet you, Rylee. And you, too, Miss Bella."

He shot a wink at the toddler and tipped his Stetson to the two women.

"Bye-bye." The little girl waved, her smile big, her face smeared with bits of ketchup. Cute kid.

"Goodbye," Gabby said, her tone soft, unsure. "I look forward to your call."

Her voice echoed in his mind all the way out the front door onto the bustling sidewalk, the mountain air brisk, but fresh from the spring thaw. The sound of Gabby's voice curled through him like the earthy scent of smoke from a campfire. Natural. Soothing. Timeless.

His memory of their attraction hadn't been exaggerated.

Truth be told, he'd thought about Gabby more than once over the two-plus years since their weeklong fling. He'd even considered reaching out to her, not that he was interested in anything long term, in spite of lectures from his dad about settling down.

Lately, his father had been especially pushy about encouraging Ryan to marry his on-again, off-again girlfriend, Nora. He couldn't seem to get it through his dad's head that they'd mostly dated whenever either of them needed a plus-one for an event, but all those society page photos of them together on social media just encouraged their parents' matchmaking.

They wanted a merger of their powerful families. Coming from the same world was a good foundation for forever—or so his folks said. Ryan had tried to shut down his father's pressure about tying the knot, except Thaddeus Taylor always brushed aside Ryan's concerns, insisting he should marry Nora and just have fun on the side.

As far as Ryan was concerned, his answer was a hard no on that. He wanted more out of his life than the business arrangement–style marriage he'd witnessed between his parents. If that's what a "shared foundation" looked like, then Ryan would rather stay single.

And since he was single, there was nothing to stop him from reaching out to Gabby.

After all, fate had dropped her in his lap yet again.

Grabbing her glass as she sat, Gabby gulped down her sparkling water, her mouth dry and closing with panic. She'd known she needed to contact Ryan. She'd been preparing herself.

Now she knew nothing could have prepared her for the first time he saw his child. Watching the two of them together, even briefly, had stolen the air from her lungs. Her hands still shook.

Fate had cut her a break, though, since he seemed to assume Bella was Rylee's child. But she couldn't count on that misunderstanding to last for long.

Exhaling a gust of breath, Rylee sagged back in her chair. "Wow, that was, uh, awkward."

"You think?" Gabby fidgeted with her silverware, moving it to the edge of her plate as if to restore order to some part of her world. "Thank you for not saying 'I told you so.'"

"Oh, honey," Rylee said as she clasped Gabby's hand and squeezed. "I would never do that."

"It's one of the many things I appreciate about you. At least it seemed like he assumed that Bella is yours, which will buy me a little time." The wheels in her mind were churning, her thoughts on an out-of-control hamster wheel. Nerves, no doubt. And over two years of stress from imagining this moment. "I can't imagine what it would have been like if he'd guessed…"

"Are you all right?" Rylee asked worriedly.

"I will be. At least now I don't have to worry about how to approach him." She passed Bella a roll, even knowing she would likely tear it up and pitch it on the floor. But she would be occupied and Gabby needed a moment to steady herself. "Thank you for going along with him thinking Bella is yours."

"Honey, of course. I can't imagine having to tell him in the middle of a public restaurant." Rylee winced, keeping her voice low as a busboy passed carrying a tray of dishes. "You'll find just the right time and place. I have faith in you."

"I hope you're right." Gabby wadded her napkin and set it beside her plate, her burger only half-finished. She'd lost her appetite right about the time a certain ghosting cowboy strutted toward her table.

Rylee smiled reassuringly. "What do you say we box this up and take Bella to the park? Make the most of the rest of the Saturday afternoon? It's a pretty mild day. She'll enjoy the fresh air."

And they would have longer to talk away from prying ears. If she chose. That was the beauty of their friendship. Rylee wouldn't push her. Just gently suggest and listen.

"Park? Play?" Bella squealed, clapping her hands.

Her excitement reminded Gabby all over again of how small their apartment was, with its postage-stamp patio and constant reminders from childless neighbors to keep quiet. She hadn't been able to give her daughter a father, much less a sprawling backyard, but for today, she could bundle her up and let her enjoy the sunshine.

Gabby exhaled a shaky breath. "Park it is, then."

Even though she wanted nothing more than to crawl under her covers and hide, she would do anything to protect her daughter's happiness—big or small. Including facing down the mighty Ryan Taylor.

Chapter Two

March in Montana was one of Ryan's favorite times of year with the earth just waking up from the deep freeze of a northern winter. Sure, the temperatures still dipped pretty low at night, but without the bitterness found in the dead of winter.

His home, this land, was in his blood. And right now he needed an evening ride with his two brothers after a stressful workday. His concentration had been shot from the surprise of running into Gabby Hammond after all this time.

Hauling his mind off the distracting memory of her silky hair, he checked his saddle's cinch. The scent of hay and leather offered a familiar comfort. Once satisfied at the fit, he called over his shoulder to his brothers, Daniel and Seth. "I'll meet you out front when you're done saddling up."

"Right behind you," said Daniel, the firstborn and a decade older than Ryan.

Seth, the second of their brood, waved from a far stall.

Reins held lightly, Ryan walked the chestnut stallion toward the wide-open barn doors framing the late-day sunset. Already, the horse's nostrils flared in excitement.

He understood the feeling. He, his brothers and their three sisters had ridden the Triple T together growing up—because they loved it but also because it provided a convenient escape from the tension between their parents and the way their misogynistic dad treated their mom. No surprise most of them were unattached given their parents' hollow marriage. Only two of his sisters were in a real relationship.

Those sibling horseback outings had become a rite of passage, like swims in the pond. Once one of them was able to ride on their own, that brother or sister was included in the grand escapes. He still recalled the day they scooped up the youngest of the family—Eloise—during a particularly "vocal" argument between their parents over his refusal to give Imogen a checkbook or credit card, instead doling out cash to her like a child's allowance. At the sound of their mother's tearful responses, Ryan had decided Eloise was ready to join. They would just go slow and put her on a pony.

The clop of hooves alerted him a moment before Daniel pulled up alongside him, astride a quarter horse. "You look preoccupied. What's on your mind?"

"Nothing I can't handle," he said dismissively, smoothing a hand over the neck of his mount. The property sprawled in front of them—from the upscale log mansion, to the pasture, then densely wooded forest reaching well up into the mountains.

Seth worked the reins on a new Tennessee Walking Horse recently added to the stable. "Is there a problem at the office? Something we should know about?"

Ryan tucked a foot into the stirrup, swung a leg over and settled, leather creaking. "Brother, you would be the first to know if there was trouble at the office— probably before me."

Clicking his horse into motion, he soaked in the panorama before him, tension and exhaustion fading like the sun slipping closer to the dip between two mountains, adding a golden glow to the first greens of spring. A chilly breeze funneled over him, the perfect jacket weather, a relief from the thick layers of winter.

He guided his Thoroughbred past the home where he'd grown up, a towering log mansion of around thirteen thousand square feet. "Home" sported about a dozen bedrooms, each suite offering privacy for the family to live together on the working ranch, the cornerstone of the family's empire. Some chose to stay at the home base; others, like himself, opted to build a house of their own nearby in the same log-mansion style.

Too bad they couldn't have had that level of isolation as kids.

Daniel scrubbed a hand over his five-o'clock shadow. "So if it's not work related, then your mood is due to a personal problem."

"Not a problem," Ryan said as they passed the pond, the site of swimming, fishing and, in the winter, ice-skating. "More of a distraction, really. I ran into someone I, uh, used to know."

Seth quirked an eyebrow. "A female someone?"

Might as well share. If he couldn't talk to them, whom could he trust? "We had a fling at a cattle convention a couple of years ago. At the end of the conference, we went our different ways."

Daniel's quarter horse started across the stream with confident, sure steps. "So if she's a distraction, does this mean you and Nora are on the outs?"

"Nora and I have never been exclusive," Ryan reminded him, clearing the rocky stream. "In spite of what Dad wishes."

Seth laughed dryly. "Does Nora know that?"

Jaw tight, Ryan nodded. "I've made my allergy to marriage abundantly clear to her. Neither of us wants anyone to get the wrong impression, given all the pressure from our parents. We all know how domineering Dad can be when he's determined to get his way."

His brothers sighed in unison, a sentiment Ryan echoed. Their dad took authoritarian to a toxic level. His misogynistic attitude had even chased off their sisters—one of whom lived on Triple T, although Eloise and Charlotte had since returned to Bronco and found lives in their hometown. Ryan hated the rift in his family and the awkwardness that blanketed gatherings when his sisters made a rare, obligatory appearance.

"So," Daniel said, "tell us more about this mystery woman who has the power to distract our commitment-phobic brother."

Ryan ignored the jab. "Her name is Gabrielle Hammond. She's a veterinary supplies rep."

"Ah," Seth said, tapping his temple, "that explains the conference hookup."

He winced at the term *hookup*. Sure, he and Gabby had gone their separate ways after, but they'd shared more than sex. They'd talked about ranching and animals, books and favorite movies. "We spent the week together."

Daniel clicked for his horse to break into a canter, picking up the pace out into an open field toward the dense pine forest on the other side, and his brothers followed suit. "And now she's here in Bronco. Since you and Nora have such a bizarre understanding, are you and this Gabrielle person going to, uh, reconnect?"

Seth snorted on a laugh. "That's one way to put it. So? What's the plan?"

"No plan as of yet. Maybe that's why I needed this ride, to clear the clutter of the workday from my mind so I could focus. She's a beautiful woman, funny, outgoing." And their chemistry had been off the charts. Right now, he couldn't think of a single reason not to see if that still applied. Making up his mind, he said, "I have been considering asking her out, offering to show her around town. She only moved here a month ago."

He didn't care what his father thought, but he did wonder about his brothers' impressions. He tipped his Stetson down lower to hide his expression, not entirely comfortable yet with how much he wanted to see Gabby again.

Daniel's brows pulled together, a glint of suspicion creeping into his eyes. "And she looked you up, after all this time, once she moved here?"

"Careful there," Seth interjected. "You're starting to sound like Dad."

"Whew," Ryan chuckled as they reached the other side of the field, guiding his horse onto a well-worn path into the woods. "That's harsh. Watch out or he'll stick your head in the toilet like he did when you ate all his Easter candy. And to answer the question, I just ran into her at the Gemstone."

Daniel nodded slowly. "She had to know you live here. Especially given what she does for a living.

And you actually think it's just a coincidence that she landed here?"

Seth held up a finger. "There you go, channeling Dad again."

Daniel leveled an oldest-brother look toward Ryan. "Keep in mind, though, that just because Dad's a jerk doesn't mean he's always in the wrong. Since she works for the veterinary supply company, there's no escaping the fact that she is very aware of the family fortune. If she's not a gold digger, then there's not a problem."

"Exactly," Ryan agreed, even as every part of him balked at the thought of her being anything but genuine. He hadn't forgotten the way they met and the surprise show of emotion he'd glimpsed. "No need to argue because it'll sort itself out. Right, Seth?"

"Sure. I guess there's something to be said for Nora after all." Seth ducked to avoid a low-hanging branch, a flock of sparrows taking flight upward. "At least you know she's not after our family's money."

Ryan shot a sarcastic glance at his brother. "Not that you're insinuating that's the only reason a woman would be interested in me."

Daniel raised a hand in defense. "Message received. I'll back off. Go ahead and call this woman if you want."

Ryan started to point out that he'd only said he planned to show her around town, but what would be the point? He knew full well he was going to ask Gabby out as soon as he returned from the ride.

Lucky for him, he had her business card with her personal cell number and he intended to make use of it once he was out of his brothers' earshot.

Gabby sat cross-legged on the floor by her daughter's toddler bed, thankful Bella had finally drifted off. Hopefully their trip to the park had worn her out enough that she would sleep deeply through the night. Because if ever Gabby had needed some alone time with her thoughts, tonight was the night.

The scent of baby shampoo and lotion, the perfume of a freshly washed child, swirled gently through the room. The white-noise machine droned with a lulling echo that drowned out the street noise outside the window. She stacked the pile of books from evening story time, everything from *Ten Little Monkeys* to start off with, then winding down with the calmer *Goodnight, Moon.*

Now, she was left alone with her own thoughts, unable to avoid memories of the encounter with Ryan earlier in the day. Sure, she'd seen him from a distance since moving here, but nothing compared to being so close she could see the pale flecks of silver in his blue eyes, eyes so like their daughter's.

Her hand slipped up to adjust the unicorn-patterned covers around Bella's shoulders, taking comfort in the rise and fall of her little chest. Countless times she'd done the same, afraid to sleep for fear something might happen if she took her attention off Bella for even a moment. The weight of solo parenting was overwhelming at times, but Bella was her everything.

The miracle of her baby girl still took her breath away. Certainly the early days had been difficult on her own. She'd worried about money, about her daughter missing having a daddy like the other kids.

About who would care for Bella if anything happened to Gabby.

Gabby had never known her own father, and her mother had passed away just after Gabby graduated from high school. She had no siblings to rely on. In the past, when she'd only needed to worry about herself, she'd filled the empty spaces in her life with work.

That was no longer an option.

And even as she knew the time had come to reconnect with Ryan, still her stomach knotted with nerves over how he would react to the news. What if he rejected Bella altogether?

The mama bear inside her roared in denial at anyone rejecting the perfection of this sweet little life.

Her phone vibrated against the floor, lighting with an unknown number. Most likely something to do with work, although it was rather late for that.

Easing to her feet, she tiptoed from the room, careful not to wake her daughter. A tiny red light on the baby monitor glowed, assuring her that the camera was operating. She ducked into the hallway just as the call ended.

She slumped against the wall by a framed Bella handprint and thumbed a quick text.

Sorry to miss your call. I don't recognize the number. Who are you trying to reach?

There. That should weed out any spam. She padded down the narrow corridor lined with photos toward the back sliding door that led to her little fenced patio garden. Her mini-Aussie could use a bit of outside time before bed.

After snagging a thick sweater off the coat tree, she stepped out into the chilly night air. A fur ball of energy, Elsie bounded outside like a racehorse out of the gate. She had lovely inside manners, but gracious, she needed more space to run than this little patch of grass. And the apartment building's rules dictated that dogs remain on-leash at all times when outside the fenced micro-patio.

She dropped into a plastic chair and checked her phone.

The typing bubble activated for a moment before a message popped onto the screen.

This is Ryan Taylor, calling for Gabby.

Her stomach lurched. Her grip around her cell tightened as she read the rest of his text. Sure, she'd given him her card but she hadn't expected him to reach out to her after all this time. And even if she harbored a small hope of him phoning, in no realm had she envisioned him doing so right away.

I sure hope you didn't pass me a card with a fake number, because I'll be very embarrassed if this is the contact info for a gas station.

Why did he have to be as charming as she remembered? For Bella's sake, she wanted him to be wonderful. For the safety of her own emotions, though? She needed him to be boring as dry toast.

She drew in a bracing breath of cold air and thumbed Redial.

He picked up on the first ring. "Do you carry diesel fuel at your station?"

She laughed lightly, albeit her voice squeaked a little from nerves. "You can also get a car wash with a fill-up."

"Thanks for calling me back." His deep voice warmed her through the speaker, somehow more intimate as she sat here alone in the dark.

Well, alone other than for Elsie, who was currently digging a hole in the middle of the microscopic yard. Gabby didn't have the heart to stop her. Some days you just had to find an outlet for the frustration.

"Well, Ryan, it's past office hours, but we can make an appointment to discuss business." She most definitely didn't intend to talk about Bella on the phone.

"Actually, I'm not calling about a ranch order." He paused for so long she wondered if he was going to continue, then he said, "I was wondering if you are free to join me for dinner tomorrow."

She straightened in her chair. Elsie dug faster.

Dinner? As in a date?

If so, he was about two and a half years too late with that offer. She didn't even want to think about what a call like this would have meant to her back then, after their fling, before she learned about the pregnancy... and even after.

That was then. This was now. And she searched for the right answer. She couldn't just show up on his doorstep with Bella tomorrow night. She knew Rylee already had plans and there wasn't another short-notice option. "Thank you, but I'm not available tomorrow evening."

While Bella went to Tender Years Daycare while Gabby worked, they didn't offer an evening option.

"When are you available?" he asked smoothly, not sounding in the least deterred.

Well, she did need to speak with him. Soon. The time to tell him about his daughter was fast approaching and her stomach was a bundle of nerves. "Perhaps we could meet for lunch this week. I could leave the office and meet you."

"So you're not telling me no. That's a good sign," he said in a low rumble. "I'm tied up during the day all week with meetings and a quick business trip. What about Friday evening? We can go out to dinner."

Another dinner invitation. She chewed her thumbnail and searched for an answer. No luck.

After five heartbeats of silence, he assured her, "Just dinner, nothing more. To catch up…"

Unless she wanted more.

He didn't need to say it. The implication was clear after what they'd shared back then.

Still, she had to accept, even if he misunderstood the reason for her yes. They had to talk. She would have preferred a private place for the conversation, given how easily this discussion could go wrong.

Although maybe being in the public eye would keep tempers under wrap. Dinner. At a restaurant. If Rylee could watch Bella, accepting his offer made the most sense.

"Let me see if I can move around some plans. I'll text you and let you know, either way." She stared at Elsie for inspiration, or distraction. Regardless, as if sensing tension leave the air, the dog stopped digging, circled the hole twice, then curled up in the shallow indention. "I really would like to speak to you."

"Good." The pleasure in his tone was flattering. "Assuming we're a go, I'll pick you up around six."

"I'll drive myself," she rushed to say. The last thing she needed was his running into Bella at her apartment and asking questions before she had the chance to explain. "Just text me the restaurant information and I'll meet you there."

"I'm looking forward to it. Good night, Gabby," he said just before the line disconnected.

As she willed her heartbeat to slow, she reminded herself it was not a date. It could never be a date. That ship had sailed. If he hadn't cared enough to return her calls two years ago, when it had mattered most, she wasn't interested in him anymore. There was nothing left except for her to figure out how to build a future co-parenting Bella.

It was just dinner. No big deal. Hadn't he reassured his brothers of that during their horseback ride?

So why had Ryan thought of Gabby repeatedly over the past week, anticipating this evening out? Wondering if she would stand him up? He couldn't miss how her request to drive herself kept him at arm's length. While he'd wanted to take her to The Association, a private dining club for well-to-do ranchers, he opted for something more midrange to put her at ease.

And thank goodness, the second he cleared the door into Pastabilities there she was, waiting for him at the hostess stand. The scent of garlic and spices teased the air.

She had changed from her work clothes, no business suit or vet supply logo in sight. Instead, she wore a cotton maxi-dress with ankle boots and a sherpa-lined denim jacket. The dark yellow fabric brought out the highlights in her hair as it flowed loosely around her shoulders. His hands clenched into fists, his fingers itching to thread through those locks and discover if the strands were as silky as he remembered.

No less than three people clapped him on the back on his way toward her, calling out greetings and asking what brought him here tonight. He wished he could have chosen somewhere farther away, where he could be anonymous, but just as in choosing a more low-key restaurant, he'd opted for closer.

He didn't want to ponder why it was so very important to win her over this evening.

"Hello," he said as he pocketed his keys, never taking his eyes off Gabby. "I hope you haven't been waiting long."

"You're early." She smiled tentatively, shifting from foot to foot nervously. "I just happened to have been a bit earlier."

He took heart at the possibility she could have been anticipating this as much as he had. "To be honest, I wondered if you were going to stand me up."

She raised an eyebrow. "That would be rude— *ghosting* a person."

Something in her tone gave him pause. But he forged ahead, cupping her elbow. "True enough. But I wondered all the same."

The hostess led the way to their table, one quietly tucked in the back just as he'd requested, lowering the chance of being interrupted. The room glowed from the flames of hurricane lamps on all the tables.

He held out a chair for Gabby. The glide of her hair over the back of his hand sent a fresh rush of memories through him. Yes, every bit as silky.

"Thank you." She spread her linen napkin over her lap.

"Have you eaten here before?"

"The place is always packed." She motioned to the full tables around them, some of the diners glancing their way with undisguised interest. "A last-minute reservation, especially for the best seating, is hard to come by if your surname isn't Taylor."

"Touché. Well, I hope you enjoy the meal. I highly recommend the chianti-braised short ribs—it's from the best locally sourced beef," he said with a grin.

"What would you say if I told you I've become a vegetarian since we saw each other last?" The teasing light in her eyes was magnified by the candlelight in the middle of the table.

Was she hoping he would argue? "I would say that's a personal choice and leaves more for me to enjoy."

"A wonderfully diplomatic answer, especially for a beef rancher," she said smartly.

He tapped the menu. "Does that mean you're having the grilled eggplant?"

She crinkled her nose. "I'm having the ribs."

He threw back his head and laughed, quieting when their waitress arrived, placing water and a bottle of wine on the table. Would Gabby realize the planning he'd put into this date?

He noticed how she sipped her water and ignored the wine. "Would you prefer a different vintage? Or something that will partner better with your meal?"

"No alcohol for me. I need a clear head," she said, then rushed to add, "I'm driving."

"I can take you home. There's no pressure in that offer. I'll be a perfect gentleman. Scout's honor." He crossed a finger over his heart.

"Were you really a Boy Scout?" She crossed her arms.

Still defensive?

"Not a Boy Scout." His father had packed after-school hours and summers with learning the ranching business. "But I do consider myself a man of honor."

Something flashed through her eyes, an emotion he couldn't define, before she quickly schooled her features again. He'd enjoyed their time together two and a half years ago. It had been lighthearted, fun. The only serious moment had been when she'd confided about her ex-boyfriend, and even that confidence had been accompanied with her vow that she wanted, needed a carefree escape.

Unfolding her arms, she traced her finger along the rim of her water glass, a light tune ringing between them. "Catch me up on your life since we saw each other last."

"Work, more work," he said, simply, then realized

he needed to offer more if he had any hope of putting her at ease. "After our time together at the cattle convention, I spent some time overseas handling a new business acquisition for my dad."

"Keep talking." Her glass kept singing softly. A nervous tic? Or was she trying to calm herself? "I'm interested."

"We were at a pivotal point in spreading the brand to a European market." He thought back to that time, how he'd hated having to end the week with Gabby, but then as he sank deeper and deeper into the work, he realized how little of himself he had left for any kind of relationship, especially a long-distance kind. "It was intense and rewarding."

"So it was successful?" The crystal tune stopped. She pulled her hand back, fingers trembling.

With nerves? Maybe she truly had been looking forward to this evening. He settled into the conversation, hoping chitchat would put her mind at ease.

"We're better established in the global marketplace now, yes." Failure hadn't been an option. He'd needed to find a niche for himself somewhat outside of his father's overlong, domineering shadow. So Ryan had turned his entire focus to the mission.

Sure, he'd thought of Gabby over the years, even considered phoning her. But bottom line, he didn't question the decision he'd made. She'd been stinging from the rejection of her boyfriend. Ryan had known he wasn't the right man to help her heal. He was a fling guy. So he'd moved on.

She toyed nervously with her necklace, the crystal on the chain looking like a birthstone. "Do you still travel a lot for your job?"

What was her birthday? He knew so little about her, but intended to learn more. "Are you asking me if I'm sticking around Bronco? I may travel for work, but this is my home."

She blinked quickly. "I'm just curious. You didn't share much about yourself back then. I didn't, either, for that matter, other than that evening I had too much to drink and told you about my ex." A wry grin tipped the corner of her pink lips. "To be fair, we didn't give ourselves much time to talk. We were both too busy."

Heat spread through him at the memory of all the ways they "hadn't talked" back then. "I'm hoping we can share more about ourselves now, since fate has brought you to my hometown."

She chewed her bottom lip, more of those nerves radiating off her. "We do have a lot of blanks to fill in. A lot has happened in the past couple of years."

"Yes, starting with… Are you seeing anyone?" he asked, caring far too much about her response. But that was the whole reason for this dinner. To pick up where they'd left off back in Nashville. Hopefully his question would reassure her of his intentions.

"No. I haven't had the time. And you?" she shot back.

A wave of relief washed over him that she was free. "I date, nothing serious. My parents are pushing me to get married. And to be honest I've seen a woman off and on for a while. Off, currently. But we're just not right for each other."

"How come?"

Heartened at her interest, he answered, "There's nothing wrong with Nora. She's a beautiful, accomplished woman. We've had some trust and honesty issues to work through. But bottom line, we just don't have that…connection."

Not like he and Gabby shared in Nashville.

A connection he wanted to rekindle. Something that wasn't going to happen if he didn't find a way to disperse the awkwardness between them. He'd done most of the talking. Maybe drawing her out about herself would help. "What about you? What have you been up to since we saw each other last?"

She looked away, her eyes darting in an unfocused way. "Uh, I've been busier than ever before."

Curious, he leaned forward, unable to read her expression. "Busy with work? I'm glad to hear your company's doing well."

"Not with work…" She twisted the cloth napkin so tightly between her fingers, they turned white. "I was raising a baby. Your baby girl."

Chapter Three

Gripping the edge of the table until her knuckles hurt, Gabby held her breath, waiting for Ryan's response to hearing that he was a daddy. Her pulse hammered in her ears until she thought her heart would explode, and she felt more than a little sick to her stomach. She hadn't meant to blurt the news about Bella quite so abruptly, but his comment about Nora and their issues with trust and honesty had her conscience stinging.

So many times over the past two years Gabby had played out the conversation with Ryan in her mind, practicing. This wasn't remotely how she'd imagined it. But nerves were chewing her up. It didn't help that he looked so mouthwateringly handsome in his jeans and sports coat. His Stetson on the extra seat reminded her of the time he'd dropped the hat on her head.

She'd been naked. So had he.

But that felt like a lifetime ago. She needed to focus on getting through the present without causing a scene in the busy restaurant full of Bronco residents. Ryan's shocked silence and steely stare led her to fill the weighty quiet between them.

"I know I should have told you about the baby sooner." The words tumbled out of her mouth until they all but piled on top of each other in a garble of defensiveness. And yet, why should she feel that way when he'd been the one who hadn't returned any of her messages? Sitting taller in her seat, she began more slowly, "But *you* ghosted *me* when I reached out to you after our, uh, *time together* in Nashville."

"Ghosted you?" His eyebrows shot up, then back down in a scowl. "I did no such thing."

He sounded sincere, indignant even, but that didn't make sense. His denial angered her all over again, stoking a resentment that had started back when she was pregnant, alone and afraid of how she would juggle single parenthood.

"I reached out to you on multiple social media platforms." She jabbed a finger at him, while keeping her voice low. "I phoned the number you gave me. And I sent letters. All with no response from you. Short of renting an airplane with a Call Me banner and flying it over Taylor Beef, I'm not sure what else I could have done."

The more she talked through the ways he'd ignored her, the more her anger increased that she had to resort to this way of communicating such monumentally important news.

He studied her through narrowed eyes. "When did you make contact?"

"Right after I found out," after a positive home pregnancy test. "I felt you had a right to know. Clearly, I still do or I wouldn't be telling you now."

"So you first reached out to me—what?—a few months after we were together?" He rubbed a hand along the back of his neck, waiting until the server passed with a tray full of pasta for the next table over, then continued, "I was overseas for that project I told you about."

"Were you on a deserted island?" she asked sarcastically.

"Hold on," he interjected with rigid control. "Let me finish. My social media got hacked while I was away. I ended up shutting it all down and starting over with a new account, with increased privacy and security. Do you think your messages may have gone to one of the fake profiles?"

His explanation gave her pause. She searched her mind for details on that time, and still she couldn't let him off the hook so easily. "It's a possibility. But it still doesn't explain the calls and letters you didn't answer. I used your office number and address. I *know* those are real because I looked them up."

His square jaw jutted. "I never received any messages or letters."

That's it? He was just going to deny ghosting her? "I'm not a liar."

Tendons in his neck flexed. "Still, you didn't tell me your story for two years. It seems odd you would choose now."

Anger fired through her. What exactly was he implying? Bella deserved better than this. For that matter, so did she.

"First you're mad I didn't inform you and now you're irritated I'm telling you now? So much for that 'connection' you claim to have felt back then, a connection so 'strong' you didn't bother to contact me even once all this time." She pursed her lips and stared back at him, their standoff lasting through the last chorus of the live guitar music.

Finally, he exhaled hard. "Fair enough. Truce?"

She pulled a smile, even though her stomach was in knots. "Truce."

Nodding, he leaned forward, elbows on the table. "So, when can I meet my daughter?"

Her maternal guard went up. Way up.

"You already did," she said simply.

She watched his face as he put the pieces together of that chance encounter last week.

He scrubbed a hand along his jaw, his face suddenly weary. "We were careful with protection. How do I know she's mine?"

Ouch. His question hurt. She bit back the urge to shout at him. But beyond the fact that they were in public, shouting would serve no purpose. For Bella's sake, they needed to get along. He had only her word for it that she and Bradford hadn't slept together in the months before their breakup. "You're the only one who could be her father."

"I'm sure you can understand that I find it tough to take your word for it, given that you and your boyfriend had only just broken up the day before we met," he said tightly, toying with the stem of his untouched wineglass. "What would you say if I insist on a paternity test?"

Not an unreasonable request, yet still sad to find herself in this position. "I'm comfortable with a DNA test, because I know it will affirm that Bella is your child."

He nodded, his handsome face chilly. "The sooner the better."

It was not even close to the response she'd been hoping for, but at least the truth was finally out there. She'd done the best she could with a horribly awkward situation. She just prayed that once he learned the truth, his feelings would soften, that he would want to be a part of their child's life—without tension that would only hurt their daughter. As if Bella wouldn't already be confused by the new man in her life. Most important of all, she prayed that Ryan would be a father worthy of their precious little girl.

Because no matter how wealthy and influential he might be, she would stand him down in a heartbeat for her child.

Cradling a drink, Ryan sat on the glassed-in balcony of his private home on the Triple T, staring into the inky darkness, searching for peace to settle the turmoil. Stars were brighter here with so little artificial illumination to compete with. He'd closed in the space with windows so he could enjoy the sensation of lying under the night sky even when work kept him from camping in a sleeping bag.

Life usually felt simpler under the constellations. And if ever he'd needed simplicity, tonight was the night. He tipped his head back against the leather chair cushion, his feet resting on an aged whiskey barrel repurposed into a side table.

No matter the outcome of that paternity test, he had reason to be angry, hurt even. There was no "happy" outcome. Either she'd kept his child away from him for two years, or she'd lied to him tonight in an attempt to pass off another man's child as his.

He stared into the amber liquid in his tumbler— and set it aside. Peace was never found there.

At least she'd gotten to the point before the main course and they'd abruptly ended the meal, leaving. Alone. Thank goodness he hadn't picked her up prior.

Driving himself, he didn't have to hide his feelings. His turmoil.

He'd nailed the accelerator and powered down the country road leading him home. His haven. Usually. The distraction wasn't working tonight.

Restless, he thumbed through his voice mails, deleting junk calls and hang-ups before he got to a genuine message.

First one was from his brother Seth. "Dad's up to something. Hit me back when you have a free minute."

His mother's shaky voice came through on the next call. She sounded a little tipsy. "Phone me, baby, when you can. It's not important. Well, it is, somewhat. Just, uh, we'll talk."

With his mom, it was tough to gauge importance, since Imogen minimized her wishes to keep the peace in the home.

The next number on the ID…from Nora. "Hey, your mother reached out to me about some get-together. I told her I would talk to you first. Get back to me when you can."

No surprise the next one was from his dad. "Your mother is planning a dinner party next Friday and she would like for all of her children to attend. Bring Nora, too, of course."

So his father was back to applying matchmaking pressure, and not too subtle at that.

Ryan jabbed Delete. He would talk to his mom, rather than deal with his father. Imogen had so little say over her life. His dad controlled the money with an iron fist. Ryan had gone so far as to ask his mother once why she put up with the way his dad acted, and she'd simply replied that Thaddeus was a complicated man and she'd made peace with the life she'd chosen. Besides, a mother would do just about anything to ensure her children's happiness…

The thought stopped him short as he cradled his cell in his palm. Were his brothers right, then, at least to a degree? Could Gabby be after his money, but for her child's sake? He hated even having the thought pop into his mind, cringing at even the possibility of sounding like his father.

Or could he have misjudged her so deeply? He'd liked her and enjoyed her company when they'd met. He'd looked forward to their date tonight, hoping to kindle the sparks they'd shared. His hand clenched around the phone.

Yet, her story about social media and missing letters did sound suspect. And they'd been careful to use protection. But man, if she was lying, she'd sure done so convincingly.

Maybe she was one of those people who could delude themselves into believing something. She'd been pretty devastated about the breakup from her boyfriend. Perhaps it had been easier to believe the pregnancy resulted from a fling rather than having to share that child with someone who'd broken her heart.

Possible, and better than being an outright liar.

In this quiet moment under the stars, he had to consider one last option. What if she was telling the truth about the child and reaching out to him? He hated to think his staff would have been that incompetent. An office administrator screening his communication while he was gone? It rankled.

Still, over two years had passed since their fling. Two years. That alone made him question if the claim was legitimate. And if it was? If he was the father of her child? She should have tried again and again until she was certain he'd gotten the message about his baby. Now, not a baby. A toddler. And he could never recover that lost time with his child—if she was in fact his daughter.

A fresh well of anger roiled inside him over the potential loss. He thought about the brief encounter with the child a week ago, trying to remember each detail about the toddler. Except he'd been so focused on Gabby, he'd only paid passing attention to the cute toddler in the booster chair. He vaguely remembered tousled dark hair and a big smile. What color were her eyes? He didn't know and for some reason, that simple fact tore him up inside.

He had to know or he would never find peace, even out here under the stars. Waiting for the DNA results would be torture. The sooner he knew, the better. He would contact his physician first thing in the morning and figure out how to fast-track that paternity test.

* * *

Clenching the steering wheel on what felt like the longest drive ever, Gabby sat in her minivan, idling in backed-up traffic. Her nerves were shot from the confrontation with Ryan at Pastabilities. Her hands were still trembling from hearing him ask that horrible question she should have foreseen.

How do I know she's mine?

She just wanted to get home, where she could pull herself together. But she'd been delayed by a wreck blocking the two-lane country road, which made the short distance back to her apartment complex last exponentially longer.

An ambulance, fire truck and two police cruisers surrounded the accident, their lights flashing a combined strobe of red and blue into the night. The demolished SUV lying sideways in the middle of the road reminded her of how fragile life could be. And how much Bella depended on her.

Finally, a police officer began waving a single lane of cars through. Easing her foot off the brake, Gabby kept well under the speed limit, taking each turn carefully on her way home to her daughter, who was being babysat by Rylee. On the one hand, Gabby regretted missing her daughter's bedtime, but on the other, she needed time to get herself together.

Starting by pouring out her heart to her new friend and praying Rylee would have just the right words of reassurance to navigate this mess.

She threw the minivan in Park outside BH247—an upscale apartment complex in Bronco Heights that catered to young singles. Not too many residents had kids. She felt lonely and a bit out of place, but this was the best location to get to and from work and Bella's daycare. The indoor and outdoor pools with their panoramic views of the mountains had been a bonus, although she wouldn't be getting much use out of the hot tub. Some of the units were in a tower, but that meant elevators, plus second- and third-floor balconies, all a challenge to manage with a toddler and multiple dog walks a day. There were a few first-floor units with a back door to a tiny yard. The cost had been higher, but she'd made the sacrifice because carrying a sleeping toddler inside got tougher with every week.

However, forfeiting even an hour of quiet naptime? Nope.

Hitching her purse over her shoulder, she thumbed the key fob to lock her van, parked between a sports car and a custom-painted truck in a row of covered spaces. Garage parking cost extra and she'd already maxed her budget on the first-floor unit with a postage-stamp-sized patio.

Thankfully, her business had covered moving expenses because she would have grieved over losing her painstakingly collected household items. Relocating was tough for little ones and she wanted to make sure Bella had the comfort and familiarity of her unicorn-themed nursery and all her toys.

And yes, Gabby had to confess she, too, was thankful to have her own things around her. Her refurbished brass bed. The paisley sofa she'd reupholstered all on her own. She wasn't materialistic, but memories meant a lot to her. The oak dining room table was all she had left from her mother.

As she reached her front door, she shivered from more than the cold night air. Something more like shock rolled over her and she took a moment to press her hand against the door panel, her eyes lighting on Bella's little hiking boots lined up to the side, covered in mud.

Gabby could all but feel her child's soft little hand clutching hers as they took their dog along the walking trail. Her throat clogged with emotion and responsibility.

Her own mom had died in a freak accident, struck by a car in a parking lot as she was picking up a cake for Gabby's high school graduation party. Since Gabby had already turned eighteen, she was too old for any kind of child services help. She was abruptly and totally on her own, trying to figure out everything from how to arrange a funeral to how to support herself.

She'd planned to live with her mom while in college and work part-time. Instead, she'd found a full-time job waitressing and enrolled in college online. It wasn't easy, but in some ways, she'd used long hours to avoid the grief and loneliness chasing her.

Losing her mom like that left her all too aware of how vulnerable Bella was. She needed Ryan to be a stand-up parent. She needed him to be a positive, loving influence in Bella's life.

Now that Gabby had finally told him, instead of feeling relieved, she felt sick to her stomach at just how high the stakes really were. But standing out here feeling sorry for herself wouldn't fix any of that.

She slipped her key into the lock and stepped inside, calling in a soft voice, "Rylee, it's just me. I'm back."

Closing the door behind her quietly, she secured both bolts, toed off her ankle boots and set aside her bag before padding into the living area.

Rylee sat cross-legged on the paisley sofa wearing sweats, an arm hooked around Elsie while the two of them watched an old rom-com with the sound so low it was all but muted. The baby monitor hummed on the end table. The screen showed Bella tucked under the covers, sleeping on her stomach. Her favorite stuffed animal—a.k.a. kitty-kitty—held close.

Patting the empty space beside her, Rylee asked, "How did it go?"

"Well, to be honest…" Gabby shrugged out of her jean jacket and flopped onto the couch with a long exhale. "It wasn't completely awful."

"That's not a ringing endorsement." Rylee winced,

her blue eyes empathetic. "It sounds like you need to vent. There's another glass for you," she said as she poured them both some wine. "Lucky for me, I don't have to drive home since we live in the same complex. I want to hear."

Thank goodness for the gift of Rylee's friendship, because Gabby didn't know how she would have managed tonight alone. "He wants a paternity test."

Yes, her voice had wobbled but she refused to cry. Elsie whimpered and clambered over Rylee to curl up on Gabby's lap. She threaded her fingers into the mini-Aussie's tricolor coat, soaking up every bit of comfort the pup offered.

Rylee reached for her wineglass, a blue paw-print charm dangling from the stem to tell the drinks apart. "I guess that's to be expected—given their family's wealth."

"I'm not interested in his money for myself or Bella." And she hated that people would even consider that. "We're managing just fine."

"Of course I know that," Rylee rushed to assure, pressing a shoulder against hers. "But he doesn't."

Hugging Elsie closer, Gabby puffed out her cheeks with an exhale. "It's tough not to feel defensive. He insists he never received my messages on social media." She explained about his hacked account.

"That makes sense." Rylee tucked a lock of auburn hair back under her brown headband. "But it doesn't explain the messages you left with his secretary or the letters you sent. Wasn't it registered mail?"

"Exactly." Gabby wished she could have pleaded her case more articulately earlier. "I told him about reaching out to his business and he all but accused me of lying."

"Whoa." Rylee eyed her over the rim of her wineglass. "I'm surprised you didn't get up and walk out. I would have been sorely tempted."

The empathy felt good on her bruised heart. "If this was just about me, I would have. But I have to think of Bella."

"True enough. What happens now?" Rylee nodded, setting her drink back on the scarred oak coffee table that bore chew marks on one corner. Bella or the dog? Gabby had never caught either of them in the act so the mystery remained.

"We take a DNA test." Heartsick, Gabby sighed, settling deeper into the throw pillows while her gaze skimmed the television screen where the happy rom-com couple celebrated their new beginning at a wedding while the credits rolled. "And while I understand, it's still…embarrassing. I never thought I'd be in this position."

She was a long way from her happy ending romantically. But she had Bella, and that was everything.

"For what it's worth," Rylee said, "no matter how this shakes out, you're not alone."

"Thank you." Gabby gathered her friend in a quick hug, heartened by the talk and the support. "That means more to me than you can know."

But even as she said it, Gabby was also all too aware of an inescapable truth. This was Ryan Taylor's town. But where did that leave her?

Chapter Four

Ryan knew his family physician had put a rush on the testing—samples taken on a Saturday, results by Monday—but the wait had been interminable.

Now, he sat with Gabby in his doctor's office, diplomas packing the walls along with awards and mountain photography. They'd agreed this wasn't news to get in the mail, and his GP had conceded to protect them from prying eyes by bringing them in through the back entrance.

Gabby sat beside him, picking at her fingernails nervously. She was back in her business wear today, a brown pantsuit this time, with a white button-down shirt. Her lanyard with her ID still rested between her breasts.

Better not focus on those curves. That's what

landed him here in the first place, seated in a hard plastic chair with antiseptic air, awaiting the outcome of a paternity test.

Leaning forward, he rested his elbows on his jostling knees. It was all he could do to keep from putting his head in his hands. Or pace. Yeah, he really needed to pace out the frustration.

How much longer until they heard? On the off chance that Bella was really his child, he would need to cultivate a civil relationship with Gabby. Might as well start now, so it seemed less calculated. "Thanks for meeting me here and letting me pick the location."

She clenched her hands against her thighs, hiding her chewed nails. "I needed you to trust the results."

"And I need to know you won't bolt after." Another reason for being together to get the news. She'd kept Bella tucked away for two years. What would stop her from doing so again? "Either way this turns out, we'll have a lot to discuss."

Her lips pressed into a thin line. "You're right, there will be much to discuss. I appreciate we are getting the news on somewhat neutral ground."

Okay, he wasn't doing as well with defusing this as he'd planned. "Did you think I would make you come to the ranch?"

"I should hope not. I can't imagine what that would feel like. Well, technically, all of Bronco is your domain. But your home?" She hugged herself as a shiver shook through her. "I just keep reminding myself this is about you since I already know the results."

"And it's about Bella." His chest went tight thinking about the innocent child caught in the middle.

"Of course." She clasped her birthstone necklace and he suspected it must be for her child. An emerald. What month was that? "She's always first in my—"

The door opened, cutting her words short, as the newest physician in the practice stepped inside. Dr. Swiftwater tucked her hands in the pockets of her lab coat as she sat on the edge of her desk. "I'm sorry you had to wait. We had an emergency with a child thrown from a horse. Lots of stitches and crying. We needed all hands on deck to keep the little one still."

"Understandable," Ryan said, his heart slugging. "Thank you for fitting us in Saturday and today."

Silently, Gabby nodded her gratitude, her hand still clutched around the necklace.

Dr. Swiftwater reached for two envelopes and extended her hand. "Ryan, congratulations. You're a father."

Ryan went numb. He must have said something. Or perhaps he hadn't. He dimly heard the physician telling them to take as long as they needed in her office. Ryan struggled to talk over the roaring in his ears as Gabby thanked Dr. Swiftwater before she stepped back out to see to her next patient.

There was no denying it.

Somehow, in spite of using protection, he had a

daughter. Gabby hadn't lied. His impression of her, then, hadn't been false. He was a dad. And for someone who didn't do commitment, this was the biggest commitment ever.

Quick on the heels of that thought, guilt sucker punched him over how his gut instinct had been to deny paternity. He cringed inwardly at how his behavior must have wounded Gabby.

He shifted in his chair and met her eyes full on. "I'm sorry for doubting your word. I don't make excuses. Just know that for Bella, I don't want there to be tension between us."

"I agree. And thank you for the apology." Her smile was wobbly.

This probably wasn't the best time to mention he'd done his level best to track down the letters she said she'd sent and no record could be found. Not that it mattered. Bella's security and happiness were his top priorities.

He also had to accept that his own silence had played a part in costing him time with his child. He'd had Gabby's contact information. Sure, it was a no-strings fling, but they had shared something special that week. He should have acknowledged that with a follow-up call. Or flowers thanking her for their time together and wishing her the best.

How different might things have turned out if he'd taken the initiative, rather than relegating her to a pleasant memory? Life could have been very different.

He wasn't ready to think about the wider issues of informing his family. One step at a time. Once they knew, the dynamic would get far too complicated. His mom would be excited—if his father let her. His siblings? He'd already had a taste of his brothers' skepticism.

And his sisters? He wasn't sure how they would react and there were already unknowns to navigate with Gabby. Although he imagined Eloise would be thrilled that little Merry now had a cousin. One thing he knew for sure, he wasn't waiting any longer to get to know his child.

"When can I see her?" He'd lost two years. He didn't intend to lose another minute.

Her grip shifted from her necklace to the strap of her purse as if she fought the urge to bolt. "I need to pick up Bella before the childcare facility closes."

"I'll go with you," he said without hesitation. Later, he would take a long solo ride and sort through the churning emotions inside him.

"I understand that you want to spend time with her right away, and I want that, too." Her voice shook. "But the daycare setting is chaotic. It's best for you and Bella to get to know each other in a calmer setting. And we did agree we had a lot to discuss."

He stuffed down his irritation at yet another delay. He couldn't afford to let anger alienate Gabby. For

Bella's sake, they needed to work together for the good of their kid. "All right, I defer to your parenting expertise on this. What do you suggest?"

"I'll pick up Bella…" Her throat moved in a slow swallow, showing just how overwhelmed she was as well, even though she had already known what the results would reveal.

"And?" he prompted.

She drew in a bracing breath. "Would you like to come to my apartment for supper?"

"Tell me the time and address, and I'll bring the food." Although given the lump in his throat, he wasn't sure he would be able to eat a bite.

As she pulled up outside her apartment complex, Gabby knew she should be happy. Ryan had accepted the news with grace. The moment she'd been anticipating and dreading for over two years had finally come to pass and she'd survived.

But instead of glad, she was depleted.

Thank goodness Ryan had insisted on bringing carryout. Because besides being drained, about all she had to offer at her place was nuggets, fries and apple slices—Bella's favorites. Gabby really needed to make a trip to the grocery store.

More than that, she needed to crawl into a tub and soak away stress for an hour—or more.

At least picking up Bella had given her time to prepare her daughter for the "new friend" she would be meeting. She wasn't sure how much Bella understood, especially at the end of a day that had left the toddler drifting off in her car seat. Even for an incredibly verbal child, this was complicated.

She gathered up her bag and opened her door, careful not to ding the silver sports car beside her. Tough to do, since the jerk had parked so close to the line. She had to angle sideways and circle to the other side to unload her daughter. At least the weather was milder today, well above freezing.

Bella scrubbed her eyes with her fists, yawning.

She unbuckled her daughter from the car seat, lifting her out and settling her on her hip. "Bella, what did you do at school today?"

"Ate sk-etti. Yum." She rubbed her tummy.

"That sounds like fun." Gabby thumbed away the smear of leftover spaghetti sauce on the corner of her daughter's mouth as she searched for the right words to prepare Bella for Ryan joining them for the evening. "Are you ready to meet our new friend coming over to have supper with us tonight?"

Her sweatshirt hood flopping off and onto her back, Bella tipped her head to the side, then looked all around. "Where's her?"

"The friend is a *man*." Definitely all man. "He's bringing us supper. Isn't that nice?"

Her daughter scrunched her nose, her forehead furrowed, her arms looped around Gabby's neck as she thumbed the key fob to close the sliding door and lock the vehicle.

How much was Bella processing? "You met him when we went out to eat with Rylee at the diner."

"Rylee?" Bella grinned. "I wuv Rylee."

"Me, too, kiddo." She adjusted the weight of her daughter on her hip and started up the paved walkway.

She'd taken two steps before Ryan's luxury SUV pulled into the lot, a vehicle she recognized from their tense dinner together.

Her stomach knotted and she hugged Bella closer. "There's our new friend now."

At least he parked politely in the middle of the empty spot, no straddling a line like the sports car jerk. Ryan stepped out, balancing a pizza box and holding two bags, all of which looked like enough food for a small army. He'd changed from his business suit into jeans, a Stetson covering his thick hair. Gulp. No question, she had a weakness for cowboys.

This cowboy in particular.

And it wasn't lost on her the magnitude of this moment with him officially meeting his child. Her mind filled with memories of the day Bella was born, of the nurse midwife placing the newborn on her chest. Looking into her baby's eyes for the first time, the connection had been instantaneous and deep. Would Ryan feel the same?

He stopped just shy of the two of them. "Hello, Gabby." Although he smiled, his blue eyes were serious, intent, focused on their daughter. "And hello, Bella."

The toddler tucked her face into Gabby's neck, peeking shyly.

Gabby smoothed the whispery brown hair back from Bella's face. "I'm sorry, Ryan. It just takes her a little while to warm up to…"

"Strangers?" he answered tightly before nodding. "It's okay. We have all the time in the world to get to know each other."

"Thank you for understanding." Gabby adjusted the toddler on her hip as she hitched up her purse and the diaper bag onto her shoulder.

Ryan shifted his groceries and the pizza to one hand and extended the other. "You've got your hands full. Can I take something?"

"Yes, please. Here are my keys." She dropped them into his hand. "This is a light day, though…as you'll soon see."

"I may have gone a little overboard, but given we both had a, uh, stressful day, I figured splurging was in order. I bought a bunch of different foods since I wasn't sure what she would eat."

Gabby couldn't miss that he was trying.

Bella looked up from Gabby's neck and pointed her fingers, as if counting. "Nuggets. Fries. Apples. Pwease."

"I happen to have just that." He smiled, but didn't move too close. "I have a toy, too."

"Toy?" Bella's eyes went wide.

"When we get inside." He angled his head toward Gabby as he walked alongside her. "I may have more than one. You can pick which you think she will like best."

Unease prickled through her at the thought of the unlimited funds he had to spoil Bella. Gabby couldn't—and didn't want to—compete in that fashion. It wasn't good for the child. But today wasn't the right time to address the issue of buying a child's affection. "You didn't have to do all that, you know, but thank you."

He nudged aside the toddler boots in front of the door and slid her key into the lock, his jaw tight. "I have some time to make up for."

Her conscience stung, but she'd already apologized as best she could and she'd yet to hear him take an ounce of responsibility for falling off the face of the earth after their week together. Although he had apologized, which could be considered an accountability of sorts…

Better to focus on her daughter. Her best interest had to come first. "Bella, what do you say we have a picnic on the patio with Mr. Ryan? It's a beautiful day."

Bella clapped her baby hands together and Gabby's heart squeezed tight in her chest. Her child's happiness was everything to her. And Ryan needed to understand that this little girl appreciated the small things in life—picnics and dandelions, a pile of crayons and a stack of blank paper. Even her colorings on the wall had a sweet simplicity to them.

Ryan Taylor might own this town, but Bella's affection was not for sale, any more than Gabby's.

Ryan had never been so nervous around a female before.

But then he'd never had dinner with his daughter before.

Dinner had been awkward, although luckily Bella hadn't seemed to notice. And she'd sure put down her fair share of nuggets.

Now, she sat curled in her mother's lap, groggy, as their dog nudged a fat ball around the small backyard. The evening temperature was dropping, but the seating area of Gabby's patio had an outdoor heater mounted high, radiating enough warmth for them to sit outside and enjoy the night sky. He'd always thought there was nothing more magnificent than a Montana night sky. But that was before he saw his child smile, the sparkle in her deep blue eyes rivaling any constellation.

The time with Bella had been a revelation. His first moments getting to know his daughter. He had to keep reminding himself she was his, because the sudden reality of it was all just…incredible. This sweet, precocious little girl was his child.

He knew he should leave and let them go to bed,

but he wasn't ready to say goodbye, not yet. "Since your arms are full, can I get you a refill on your lemonade?"

He'd picked up supper at Bronco Brick Oven Pizza, a deluxe along with sides of wings, salad, cheesy breadsticks and two different kids' meals.

"I'm fine." She sipped the last bit of the raspberry lemonade. "Thank you for supper. I would have scavenged something, but it's been a…draining day."

"To say the least." He felt gutted. "I put the leftovers in your refrigerator while you were changing Bella into her pajamas." The kid looked too cute in her footed pink onesie, wrapped in a blanket.

"And the gifts are perfect," she said with what looked like a begrudging smile. "By perfect, I mean not too extravagant."

"For now," he said softly, already thinking of the pony he intended to buy for her. But for today, he was glad he played things right, opting for simple presents like a little stuffed horse, a cowgirl hat and a watercolor storybook. "You've made a great life for her here."

She eyed him suspiciously. "Is that why you agreed to come to my apartment? To be sure she's safe?"

Her question caught him off guard. "Not in the way you mean. It's not wrong to want to see her room, her toys, to get to know her routine."

"Sorry," she said with an apologetic smile, shaking her head to clear away the hair falling in her face.

"I didn't mean to sound defensive. I'm just not used to sharing her."

He stifled the kick of anger and tucked her hair behind her ear. "You need understand that I'm all in." The air snapped between them, the backs of his fingers lingering on her soft cheek for an instant too long before he pulled away. "More than just an occasional shared dinner. I want to be a part of her life. I want to be her—"

Gabby held up a finger to her plump lips. "Tonight's not the night to use that word. Not yet."

"She's sleeping." Sort of.

"Trust me." Gabby cradled her daughter closer. "She's listening and soaking up every word."

Bella looked up, holding the new stuffed pony in her fist, her eyes sleepy, her voice clear as she parroted, "Trust me."

Gabby raised her eyebrows. "See? What did I tell you?"

"Fair enough," he said with a laugh. "I'll take my cue from you on when to say *D-A-D*."

"Thank you."

Was it his imagination or had her arms tightened around Bella? Had she inched farther away as if to put distance between them? Even the scruffy little dog padded over and stretched out on the ground as if staking her claim, head on her paws with wide watchful doggy eyes.

Ryan stifled a painful twinge, remembering his

parents' tug-of-wars over their six children. And how would they take the news of becoming grandparents?

He definitely wanted to delay that for a while longer. "What time do you want me to pick you and Bella up tomorrow for lunch?"

"Tomorrow?" she asked, looking startled.

"There's a great restaurant—The Library. Are you familiar with the place?"

"I won a gift certificate there in the Valentine's Day bake-off at Bronco Motors last month." Already she was shaking her head. "But I'll have to pass on your invitation. I'm glad it worked for you to be here tonight, but I have plans—for Bella and for me. I'm taking her with me on a work errand donating some extra veterinary supplies to Happy Hearts Animal Sanctuary."

Her rambling explanation sounded more like a stall tactic. They'd both known about hearing the DNA test results today. She had to have realized he would want to spend time with Bella. "I'm familiar with the sanctuary. My cousin Daphne runs the place."

"Daphne Cruise?"

"Daphne *Taylor* Cruise." The sanctuary housed horses, cows, pigs, goats, ducks, rabbits and assorted cats and dogs—all of which Bella would no doubt love.

She smoothed a hand over her daughter's tousled brown curls. "Are you related to everyone around here?"

"A good many of them." As difficult as his father was, Ryan couldn't imagine not having his big extended family around him.

"Back to our discussion about tomorrow," she said primly. "After the sanctuary, I will be driving over to the animal shelter in Tenacity. My company has some surplus and samples to donate."

Even though she was pushing him away, he was moved by her thoughtful spirit. Tenacity was a small, rural, down-on-its-luck town. "Sounds like a busy, fulfilling day with plenty to entertain Bella. I'll take the day off and drive you. We can finish up with dinner at The Library."

Had his words sounded pushy? Well, he figured he was owed a little grace today after finding out he'd missed nearly two years of his daughter's life.

Bella rubbed the mane on the toy pony between her fingers like a talisman. "Li-berry?" Her head popped up at that last word. "I wanna book."

Gabby angled a quick glance at Ryan. "I started taking her to story time before she could even sit up. I may have gone a bit overboard as a first-time parent." She rested a hand on Bella's head. "Sweetie, it's a food place, not a book place."

"Princess, if it's okay with your mom, we could go to the bookstore, too." He met Gabby's eyes over Bella's head, hoping he hadn't overstepped. "What time should I pick you up?"

She studied him so long he thought she would put

him off regardless. Then she sighed, and he knew he'd won. Yet, the victory felt shallow, because in spite of his competitive spirit at work, he wanted something very different for his child. He just needed to learn more about Gabby to figure out how to make that happen.

Chapter Five

Her morning had *not* started off on the right foot and Gabby sure hoped that wasn't a sign of trends to come during this daylong outing with Ryan and their daughter.

She'd overslept, which meant no time to dry her hair. Her coffeepot had broken. And she'd forgotten to swap the clothes out of the washer the night before.

Now, she sat in the passenger seat of Ryan's SUV with a damp, messy hair bun and a caffeine-withdrawal headache. She was stuck wearing her old, faded blue jeans and a sweatshirt with the company logo, which was fine for the casual work she had planned for the day. But was it so wrong to want to look her best around the man who'd walked out of her life two and half years ago?

Bella hummed in her car seat behind her as her favorite cartoon about musical unicorns played on the vehicle's built-in video system.

As they powered deeper into the grazing and farm land, she had to admit that she appreciated having Ryan drive. She was used to mountains, having lived in Tennessee, but this region of Montana still felt so untamed and remote, she brought maps with her because she feared her GPS would lose signal. Heaven forbid that she might have to use a compass to get home—or if she ran out of gas.

Not that she should be surprised at the topography. *Montana* meant *mountainous* after all. The place was rugged and majestic, much like the man beside her sporting denim and dusty boots.

Gulp. "Thank you for driving us today. It's beautiful out here." Especially with the sun shining all the brighter through the unpolluted sky. "But this is more remote than I realized."

"And thank you, it's a pleasure that I get to spend the day with Bella." His blue eyes, so like their daughter's, swept up to the rearview mirror that showcased an image of the toddler, wearing fuzzy, pink headphones, her gaze locked on the images flickering across the screen. "How much do you know about the sanctuary?"

"The basics." She smoothed her palms over the soft knees of her jeans while she watched a field of cattle graze nearby. "That it's an idyllic property providing a home for cats and dogs and all sorts of displaced animals."

"All true," he confirmed, turning off onto a narrow dirt road, a sign on the corner pointing the way to Happy Hearts Animal Sanctuary. "The place has an interesting history. There's a rumor that the property is haunted, due to a long-ago barn fire that killed a cowboy, his girlfriend and a number of horses."

"Oh my. How tragic." She pressed a hand to her chest, glad that Bella had her ears covered. "I'll be sure to keep my eyes open for ghosts. Pretty ironic that Daphne's husband runs a ghost tour business—or maybe that's not a coincidence at all."

As she looked at the rescue through the windshield, the sprawling place had a timeless aura that invited images of wandering specters. Nestled in the rolling foothills, the sanctuary sported a main house, several barns and numerous fenced-in areas for the different animals.

She loved her job, but wow, she wouldn't mind spending time somewhere like this. Seeing the animals flourish had to be so rewarding. In college, she'd been riveted by courses in equine welfare and management, livestock development and veterinary science.

Ryan's cousin Daphne was definitely living an animal lover's philanthropic dream. As they pulled up in front of the main barn, Daphne trekked out toward them, wearing a lined plaid shirt over a hoodie, jeans and brown work boots.

She'd met Daphne before in town, and now that she knew of the Taylor family connection, she could see the resemblance. Fast on the heels of that thought, she realized that these legions of Taylors in Bronco were Bella's relatives, as well. A simple fact, but mind-blowing all the same, especially for someone like Gabby, who'd grown up with no one except her mom.

Bella squealed in excitement, tugging her head-phones off and flinging them to the floor. She drummed her tiny hiking boots against her seat. "Doggies, cows, ponies, uni-corn."

Ryan chuckled softly on his way out to jog around the hood and open Gabby's door with an old-school kind of manners she remembered well from before. Nice, but she was more interested in how he treated Bella.

"Thanks—" Gabby began, only to but cut off short by Daphne calling out to them.

"Welcome, Gabby." Daphne waved, a baby goat tucked in one arm against her chest, her work boots crunching on gravel as she approached. "I can't wait to show you and Bella around. And hello to you, cousin. I'm surprised to see you here."

Ryan thumbed the key fob, the back hatch sweeping upward to reveal stacks of boxes. "I offered my help in transporting the goods."

Gabby unbuckled Bella and hitched her onto her hip, the gentle afternoon breeze rustling the branches overhead. "I appreciated his help finding the place, but now that I know the way, I can't wait to come back again."

Undisguised interest shone in Daphne's eyes. "Well, Ryan, that's mighty nice of you."

Ryan hefted up the first of the boxes marked for the sanctuary. "Just showing Bronco hospitality. How's Evan?"

Daphne twisted her wedding band around and around on her finger. "As wonderful as ever. Still feels like we're newlyweds, even though we've been married for more than two years." Quirking an eyebrow, she elbowed her cousin. "Marriage isn't so bad. You should give it a try sometime."

Gabby started to tell Daphne that there was nothing between them, absolutely *nothing* to gossip about to all her Taylor relatives. Except there was something between them. Something big. News that would rock the family. She just wasn't ready for the big reveal yet.

Plastering a big smile on her face, Gabby said, "All right, then, shall we start unloading the boxes? I've included some freebies in addition to your order and some samples of new products."

Daphne touched her lightly on the shoulder. "Ryan can take care of unloading. How about I show you and Bella around the sanctuary so you can meet all the animals? Bella, would you like to pet the baby goat?"

Bella popped her thumb out of her mouth. "Yes, tank you."

Daphne cradled the gray furry goat as Bella stroked him with two little fingers. "And, Bella, we just got the most adorable new pony."

"Pony?" Bella wriggled to climb down from her mother's arms. "Pony, pwease."

"Right away, little miss. Follow me." Daphne gestured toward the barn.

Gabby glanced back over her shoulder at Ryan, busy at work, then surrendered to the tour. Yes, for her daughter, but also because she was curious and needed a breather from a certain cowboy's allure.

Sun peeked between the puffy clouds, streaming through oak and evergreen branches. The fields were greening with grass, although the area around the barns was a mix of packed earth and gravel from the traffic of hooves and paws.

The place was immaculately kept, especially considering all the animals on the property. Raised wooden cages housed rabbits. A screened-in "cat-io" housed about a half-dozen felines, with a separate section holding a mama and her kittens. Gabby smiled at the livestock symphony of clucking chickens and a neighing donkey.

Daphne set the goat into a pen with another and a mama, before stepping into a stall with a squat Shetland pony. "This is Buddy."

Gabby inched closer, giving Bella careful access to stroke the insanely thick mane.

"Hi, Buddy," Bella crooned, a natural around the animals, the instinct in her blood perhaps.

Leaning an elbow on the stall's half wall, Daphne said, "Your daughter is precious."

"I know how lucky I am." Love filled her heart for the cherished gift of this child. "I appreciate your taking the time to show her around."

"Of course." Daphne waved aside the thanks. "To be honest, I'm also curious. It's not often that my cousin takes a day off work for anyone. You must be special."

Her daughter was the draw. Except that wasn't something Gabby could say so she let Daphne continue with the misunderstanding—for now. "We met a while back at a conference and like he said, he's showing me around the area."

"With your cute kid," Daphne said pointedly, pulling down a sack of chicken feed and waving for them to follow. "A man only does that if he's interested."

"He's a good guy." A benign answer that didn't appear to be fooling anyone.

Daphne scooped up a handful of the feed and tossed it into the fenced chicken pen, encouraging Bella to follow suit. "He's a dyed-in-the-wool bachelor."

There was no missing the warning in the woman's voice. Gabby had trotted out the same cautions to herself. "I'm well aware that he's a player."

"I'm not sure I would use that word." Daphne knelt beside Bella to assist with the chicken feed, a seamless multitasker as she continued the conversation. "*Player* has a deceptive connotation. He's always up-front with the women he's in a relationship with."

She needed to nip this conversation in the bud before Ryan finished unpacking. It was embarrassing enough even when he wasn't around to overhear. "Thank you for the concern. I can look after myself." That part was true. "There's nothing to see here."

For now. Daphne let the topic drop gracefully, turning her attention to Bella and the chickens. Yet Gabby knew the woman's questions weren't the end of the Taylor family interest in her. Soon enough, she would be facing the scrutiny of the whole town, something she hadn't considered when bringing Bella here to meet her father.

Ryan had learned something crucial today.

There was no such thing as a schedule for parents when carting around a toddler. After they'd left the sanctuary, Bella fell asleep in the car and they had to wait until she woke up before dropping off supplies at the Tenacity Animal Shelter. Gabby warned it would ruin her mood for the rest of the day if she didn't finish the nap. Playing with the puppies and kittens had run long, for obvious reasons, then Bella had needed a snack. So they were killing time eating fries before going into the bookstore—as promised when Bella misunderstood about The Library restaurant.

Bronco City Park, with a swing set and benches, was across the street from the corner indie bookstore. Now Bella didn't want the fries, begging to swing instead.

When Gabby had started to protest, Ryan shook his head. This didn't seem like the right time to stir trouble. He could tell his decision irritated Gabby, but he wasn't ready to be a bad-guy disciplinarian.

So he pushed the swing again and again, getting a real workout while Gabby sat on a bench answering work emails on her cell, sunshine glinting the highlights in her dark hair. Across the park, he thought he spotted the elderly Winona Cobbs walking across the street with her fiancé, Stanley Sanchez, but luckily the longtime lovebirds didn't seem to notice him. A class of elementary students was doing some kind of field trip, eating their bagged lunches. Funny how he'd never really noticed the movement of kids in the world before.

Bella held the chains as she sat in the safety bucket seat, looking back over her shoulder at him. "Wanna puppy."

The little beagle mixes at the shelter had been cute as pie, and he'd been tempted. But ultimately, he'd bitten his tongue, because he was ready to get one and offer to keep it at his place. He had the land, the resources. But he sensed it wouldn't be quite that simple since Bella didn't understand his role in her life yet.

Gabby's gasp drew his attention. Her eyes went

wide and she set aside her phone. "We have a puppy, sweetie. Elsie is our puppy. We don't have space for *two* puppies."

"Two puppies?" Bella held up two fingers, having practiced for her birthday coming up.

Gabby's shoulders sagged with a weight of responsibility he'd seen often worn by his mom. "Sweetie, we live in an apartment. One puppy is all we're allowed."

Her little face scrunched. "Puppy sad."

Yep, it had been heart tugging leaving those little ones behind. When Gabby wasn't looking, he'd made a fat donation to the rural shelter. Tenacity was already such a struggling community. Now, he realized that Bella also felt the urge to *do* something, like her mother.

He didn't know a lot about kids, but he understood enough to realize that level of empathy was special in a child so young. Gabby was definitely doing something right as a mom.

"Bella?" He stepped in front of her so she could see his face and he slowed the swing by clasping her feet. "What do you say next time we go get a bunch of food and toys for these puppies? They can play with them until they get boys and girls of their own to play with. Then they won't be sad."

Bella nodded fast, a smile spreading over her windchapped cheeks. "Okay. Puppy toys."

And as he held those little shoes in his hands, he

felt his throat close with emotion and his heart crack open to let this little child crawl inside. For a man who'd prided himself on his cool logic, never had objectivity felt further away than right now, a time in his life where he would be faced with the most crucial decisions about how to handle his future as a father.

When Ryan had said he intended for them to spend the day together, in the back of her mind, Gabby had figured he would wear out and stage a work emergency. But she had to hand it to him, he was hanging in there, keeping the promised bookstore stop even though it meant they were going to be late for their dinner reservation.

There was no rushing in a bookshop, the scent of paper and coffee mixing with the aura of escapism found in the pages. She held back as Ryan knelt beside Bella, pulling one book after the other off the shelves for her to choose from.

She was surprised at how quickly Bella had taken to him, a stranger. He was being patient, but then he'd only been at this parenting gig for a day. He hadn't confronted a full meltdown over ketchup on her nuggets yet. Or the inconsolable moment when soap got in her eyes while washing her hair.

Ponies, puppies and book shopping were easy.

Familiar voices from the next aisle over interrupted her thoughts just as a couple stepped around the endcap and into sight. She recognized lovebirds Robin

Abernathy and Dylan Sanchez walking hand in hand down the book aisle, drinking coffee. She had enjoyed the brief exchanges she'd shared with the leggy blonde, a small business owner who sold horse therapeutics. And Robin's guy was down-to-earth, a new ranch owner who also ran Bronco Motors car dealership. They had the world at their feet and it was hard not to be envious of how easily love had come to them. Or so it seemed.

From the light of recognition and curiosity in their eyes, Gabby knew there would be no easy getaway. She just hoped they didn't ask awkward questions.

Robin nudged Dylan's shoulder with her own. "Ryan? What a surprise to find you here, with…a kid."

Ryan looked up quickly, a stack of storybooks in his hands and more in a discard pile by his feet on an alphabet rug. Was his handsome face turning red?

"Uh, hello. This is Bella. Her mother—Gabby—is right over there shopping." He pointed toward her. Their eyes held for a moment before he stood and continued, "Gabby and I met through her work selling veterinary supplies to the ranch."

Dylan nodded. "She was the one who won a year's worth of mechanical work at my car dealership, along with a gift certificate to The Library during Bronco Motors' Valentine's Day bake-off last month."

Robin hooked arms with Dylan, her wheat-colored

ponytail swinging. "Why don't you three join us for supper? We're going to LuLu's for barbecue."

A no-frills establishment with wooden picnic tables, buckets full of peanuts and paper towel rolls, LuLu's was housed in a former blacksmith and livery building. Any other time, Gabby would have enjoyed it, but today? She let her eyes speak a big *no* to Ryan and she prayed he would understand. She wasn't ready to field more questions about her relationship with Ryan yet.

"Next time, perhaps," Ryan said diplomatically. "We're actually on our way to dinner. We have reservations at your sister's place, Dylan."

Was he trying to stir the rumor mill, somehow put his stamp on her and on Bella? Her face started stinging with a blush of her own. Was that what today was about? She hated the suspicion creeping into her mind. But after growing up with an absent father, then being dumped so unceremoniously by Bradford, she had trouble putting her faith in a man. Ryan sure hadn't helped his case.

Dylan clapped a hand on Ryan's shoulder. "We won't keep you, then. Camilla has created a quite a buzz with The Library. You won't want to be late to your reservation. Good to see you, Bella, Gabby." He nodded from one to the other as Robin fanned a wave goodbye.

Gabby exhaled a gust of air she hadn't even realized she was holding and sank onto a small kiddie table, her hand resting on a tiny wooden chair.

Ryan scooped up the stack of children's books and clasped Bella's hand. "Come on, nugget. I hear there are cake pops at the restaurant."

Ah. He'd already learned the power of the bribe to get a kid moving.

He came up alongside Gabby, nodding toward the novel in her hand. "Are you ready to check out?"

"Oh, uh, sure." She pushed back to her feet, Bella walking between them looking for all the world like part of a family unit—which made her eyes burn with unshed tears. "I'm not so sure about supper. Haven't we already given the gossip mill enough fodder for one day?"

His jaw flexed with tension. "It won't be a secret for long so what does the gossip matter? The sooner Bella becomes comfortable around me, the easier it will be when the talk starts."

What he said made sense. Still, what if they were pushing things too quickly? "Aren't you tired of us yet? It's really okay to put off the dinner part for another time."

She needed to shore up her defenses after all the ways this day had picked away at them. Even though she'd spent months anticipating how telling Ryan about his child would play out, she'd never once envisioned an aftermath where he inserted himself into her life as much as Bella's. Which had been short-sighted of her. Foolish, even. But she'd forgotten the magnetic effect of his presence. The draw she felt toward him even though she knew it couldn't lead anywhere.

Even now, Ryan stared her down with that thrilling blue gaze as he tilted his head and asked, "Don't you and Bella have to eat?"

The simplicity of the question confused her. "Of course."

"So do I," he said as he plunked their purchases down on the checkout counter next to a bookmark display and a bowl of mints. "Call it a family dinner."

Family? Her gut clenched.

His wink and grin were familiar, making the air crackle with the same electricity that had made her melt back in Nashville—and eventually left her with another bruise on her already battered heart. For Bella's sake, she needed to remember that the next time he turned on that charming smile. They were only spending time together now for their daughter. If he was being nice, it was only about smoothing the waters between them—for Bella.

She couldn't indulge in a repeat of what they'd shared in Nashville. There wasn't any room for another no-strings hookup between them.

Even if she still found him the most charismatic man she'd ever met.

Chapter Six

Ryan hadn't been this tired since he last pulled an eighteen-hour day branding cattle. Who knew a cute-as-pie tiny toddler could drain every ounce of energy out of a person?

He held the door open to The Library, a midpriced restaurant with trendy, contemporary food. The soaring ceilings and repurposed shelves preserved the vibe of the original structure, making for a unique dining environment.

And Dylan Sanchez had been right in noting that his sister's establishment in Bronco Valley was a hit, currently wall-to-wall with diners. There was a line just to speak with the hostess, a harried college-aged girl holding a tablet.

Gabby nibbled her bottom lip, looking around with

worried eyes as she jostled Bella on her hip. "I'm feeling decidedly underdressed. And are you sure they haven't already given our table away?"

"You look beautiful and there's no need to worry about being turned away. The place is owned by my cousin Jordan's wife. If there's any need to work something out, I know she'll take care of us." He reached for Bella, but the toddler clung tighter to her mom, suddenly shy. Because of the packed space? How long would it be before his daughter looked to him for comfort, as well?

"Your cousin Camilla, right?" Gabby swayed from side to side in time to the music piping through the sound system, which seemed to soothe Bella as they waited for the line to shuffle forward. "But wait, I thought she was Dylan's sister?"

"Yes, and she's my cousin's wife. I know all the connections around here can be confusing."

"Another relative. I'm going to need a notebook of charts to keep everyone in this town straight." She rolled her eyes with a laugh. "For an only child like me who grew up with a single mom, it's a lot of connections to remember."

He couldn't imagine such a solitary life. At least he could assure her that she and Bella would never be alone again without support. He was a man of honor. They were now his responsibility. "As I said before, Bronco's a tight-knit community, but I like to think we're open to new people. You and Bella are a part of that now."

He needed to ensure his daughter knew her extended family. Felt supported by them. The force of that need surged through him with surprising strength.

"But how are they going to feel when they learn about our past? Will all the people we've seen today feel—" she paused to whisper "—betrayed? I don't expect we can keep this a secret long, but Bella needs more time."

"Soon," he said, wishing there was a way he could ease the transition for everyone. "I don't want her to be overwhelmed, either, and once word gets out… Well, you can imagine how many people from those charts will want to include her in family gatherings."

Family. The word had taken on a new and deeper meaning for him in the past couple of days. Maybe he could ask one of those familiar faces to let them cut the line.

"Yoo-hoo, cousin," Camilla called, weaving past the sea of waiting patrons, looking happy but harried in simple black pants, a white shirt and an apron around her waist. Her dark hair was swept back in a French braid. "Sorry to keep you waiting. One of our cooks called in sick and I've been pulling extra duty in the kitchen—which I love—but what a time to be shorthanded." She laughed, fanning her face with her hands.

"The curse of success," he said, his stomach grumbling softly. He tried not to be rude by looking at his watch, especially since they were late.

Camilla pivoted and patted Bella on the back. "And, Gabby, congratulations again on winning last month's Valentine's bake-off."

Gabby smiled graciously, even though she must be exhausted and hungry, too. "Winning was a delightful welcome to Bronco. You and your brother were generous with the prizes—a dinner gift certificate and a year's worth of car service? What more could anyone ask for?"

Dinner and an oil change sounded so simple to him, but meant the world to her. He forgot sometimes what a privileged world he'd grown up in.

Camilla tucked her head into Bella's field of view. "Would you like a coloring book and some crayons?"

Shyly, Bella popped her thumb out of her mouth. "Tank you."

Gabby motioned toward the open-concept restaurant. "If the food is even half as wonderful as this space, I'm in for a treat."

Camilla pressed a hand to her chest over her name tag. "That means more to me than I can say. When I was a college student, I waitressed at DJ's Deluxe and dreamed of owning my own restaurant."

"Wow," Gabby said with raised eyebrows, "I waitressed while in college, as well. It's hard work."

He hadn't known that about her. There was so

much they both needed to learn about each other if they intended to make this work for Bella.

Camilla nodded in commiseration. "I'm not afraid of sweat equity. I didn't grow up with a Taylor family silver spoon. My father is a postal worker." She stopped short, waving a hand. "I'm babbling. Give me a minute and I'll see what I can work out for a table."

Ryan winced. He prided himself on his timeliness, an essential part of professionalism. But he was late arriving to the restaurant and didn't feel right not owning up to that. Of course, how could he have cut short Bella's enthusiasm about the books? Even though his stomach was chewing on itself. "I know we're late and our table is likely gone."

"I'm sorry, but it is," Camilla said sincerely. "If you're okay waiting for just a little bit, I'll figure—"

Gabby leaned closer, the lavender scent of her shampoo drifting toward him. "Maybe it would be best if we do takeout? Bella's had a full day."

Ryan hoped Gabby wasn't trying to shuffle him off, although he could see the wisdom in cutting the day short. Sitting still in a restaurant like this would be a struggle for an exhausted toddler. He hadn't considered that when he'd chosen the location. Someplace like Bronco Burgers or LuLu's would have been a better fit after all. Maybe he should have accepted Dylan and Robin's invitation instead of being so locked into his own plan. Today was about what Bella would enjoy, not his preferences.

Camilla sighed with relief, her face full of gratitude. "I can make that happen right away. I'll put your order in immediately and toss in some complimentary chorizo-stuffed mushrooms."

"Mommy," Bella whispered urgently. "Gotta go potty."

The toddler wasn't potty-trained yet, but asking to go was a request that couldn't be denied. Although most likely they would just hang out together in the stall with nothing happening. Then Bella would argue about washing her hands, choosing instead to simply play with the soap dispenser.

With a chagrinned smile, Gabby said, "I'll be right back. Ryan, would you go ahead and place our order? I checked the menu online earlier."

"Of course," he said.

"Shrimp and corn empanadas for me and a cheese quesadilla for Bella." She smiled hurriedly. "Thank you."

Gabby hustled double time toward the ladies' room, just about setting a land speed record. He couldn't stop his smile as he watched her, her hips twitching and her ponytail swishing. He thought about earlier when she'd taken down the hair piled on her head and wrapped a band around it instead. He'd been mesmerized then.

And now.

Camilla clucked her tongue as her gaze followed his. "Cousin, you aren't fooling anyone with that story of showing Gabby around town. Good luck."

Good luck? He suspected he was going to need it to win over both Hammond females, something that grew increasingly important to him with every moment together.

As she washed her hands in the restaurant bathroom, Gabby was nervous about sharing another meal with Ryan, family style, especially when her defenses were low from exhaustion. The day had been full physically and emotionally. Still, the decision to get carryout had been easy, to avoid a meltdown from Bella.

Gabby hefted up her child. "Wash your hands now, sweetie."

Her daughter pumped the dispenser, cupping the stream of pearly cleanser. Her little forehead scrunched in concentration as she rubbed her palms together before shoving them under the warm water.

"Good job, kiddo," Gabby praised, relieved.

The far stall opened and, reflected in the mirror, Gabby saw an elegant woman step out. Gabby stifled a gasp at the familiar face. The woman had been all over Ryan's social media posts, clinging to his arm.

Nora, the old girlfriend whom Ryan broke up with because of trust issues.

Gabby wanted to run. But Bella was pumping

more soap into her palm, so there wasn't an easy escape.

Oozing confidence and wealth, the socialite clearly never had to bargain shop for a beautician and skip appointments when her budget came up short. Nora had such a put-together air about her, from her sleek hair down her back to the cut of her designer dress and expensive handbag.

Gabby was all too aware of her faded jeans and work hoodie, not to mention how her messy bun from earlier had been downgraded to a messy ponytail sometime midafternoon. She focused on getting the generous—very generous—glob of cleanser off her daughter's hands.

Nora waggled her manicured fingers under the faucet and met Gabby's gaze in the mirror. "Hello, I'm Nora. And you are...?"

Uh, the woman wanted to make small talk? No thank you. "I'm Gabby."

Hopefully she would take the hint. Wasn't there a rule about not talking to someone in the restroom? She'd heard men had that rule. Maybe she should start that as a social media trend. No chitchat in the powder room.

Nora squirted a delicate droplet of soap on her fingertips. "I saw you with Ryan out there. So are the two of you an item?"

Gabby's irritation turned to outright anger at the woman's audacity. Did she intend to turn this into a confrontation? Gabby's hold tightened protectively around her daughter.

After a day of that same question asked or implied so many times, her nerves were on edge. The fact that the question came from a woman in Ryan's life made things all the more awkward. On the positive side, she'd had a lot of practice answering this query today. "Ryan and I met a while back at a conference— cattle business. This is just, uh, a friendly outing. I'm new in town."

"With your child?" Nora shook her head, her hair falling perfectly back in place. "I can't think of when I've seen him hanging out with a toddler."

Gabby wasn't sure what to say about that, and his lack of experience with kids was something she would definitely mull over later. For now, she settled for saying, "I guess he never met a kid as charming as mine." She set Bella on the counter and plucked a paper towel for her. "Right, kiddo? Ryan is our friend."

"Friends?" Nora shut off the water and swiped her elegant fingers dry with a paper towel. "Ryan never looked at me the way he looks at you—and I was most definitely not just a friend."

Did they have to have this conversation here? Now? And why did Nora have to block the path to the door? Gabby felt trapped—and yes, jealous and insecure, and she hated those emotions. She knew better than to measure self-worth in terms of looks and money.

And her anger level ratcheted up at being spoken to this way in front of her baby girl. Bella might not understand all the words, but kids understood tone. Body language.

The realization forced Gabby to relax her shoulders and answer calmly, "I'm not sure how to respond, Nora, since it seems you've already made up your mind." There wasn't much she could say right now, especially when heaven only knew who else in this so very intermingled town might be eavesdropping from a stall. Who did this woman think she was?

"A word of warning." Nora reached behind her to clasp the door handle. "That rarefied, wealthy world of the Taylor family can be tough for an outsider."

Gabby couldn't miss the implication. Nora was not an outsider. But she was.

Without another word, the woman pushed through the door and disappeared from sight as it swung closed behind her, leaving behind an air of expensive perfume and a host of questions.

Bottom line, however, Gabby couldn't help but feel sorry for the woman. Because once Nora learned Ryan had a child, the situation would be even more uncomfortable. Gabby knew all too well how charming the man could be.

Although that didn't mean she wanted to cross paths with Nora again anytime soon. Better to hang out in the bathroom awhile longer until she could be sure Nora had cleared out.

"Sweetie, let's wash our hands again. We forgot to sing 'Happy Birthday' to make sure we cleaned them long enough."

Ryan wondered what in the world was taking Gabby and Bella so long in the restroom. He'd already picked up their order, paid and now waited by the front door. Given the steady stream of customers, Gabby had been right to opt for carryout.

His mouth watered at the spicy scent emanating from the bag, Gabby's empanadas, Bella's cheese quesadilla and the mushroom cheeseburger he'd chosen for himself.

"Ryan?" a female voice drifted past the couple shrugging into coats beside him.

Nora. Talk about crummy timing.

Even though he and Nora were no longer seeing each other, he would need to talk to her about Bella and Gabby eventually, but not now. "Nora, great to see you. What brought you here this evening?"

"I'm having dinner with some old college roommates." She flicked a sleek lock of hair over her shoulder. "And speaking of friends, I ran into your two new little friends in the ladies' room. I noticed the three of you together when you walked in."

Her saccharine-sweet tone set off alarms in his brain and her smile was so tight her bright red lips thinned. What had happened in there? And more importantly, had she said something to upset Gabby?

Or worse—Bella? His protective instincts surged.

"Nice of you to say hello," he said benignly, reining in his temper at the thought of anyone upsetting his daughter. "I won't keep you. I see your tablemates over there and I think one of them is checking to see if you want a drink."

She clicked her fingernails against each other, a mannerism he recognized as a nervous tic when she had something she wanted to say that was better left unspoken.

Finally, she shook her hands loose. "Right, and while I'm at it, maybe I'll get one for your date. After our little talk, she sure looked like she could use one." She fanned a wave. "Bye, now."

His empty stomach sank. He'd worked his tail off to make progress with Gabby today and now it could well have imploded in the span of one trip to the powder room. He was five seconds away from charging into the women's restroom to check on Bella and Gabby when they stepped out, slowly. Cautiously, even. Gabby's eyes darted around the lobby as if searching for someone other than him. Checking to make sure Nora was gone? Maybe he was being paranoid.

But he didn't think so.

Something Nora said in there had definitely upset

her. The temperature in Gabby's eyes had dropped. Significantly.

Then she glanced his way and closed the distance between them. Their eyes met. Held. Sparked, the chill turning to heat. The pulse in her neck quickened even though it was clear she was still annoyed.

An answering warmth kindled within him in spite of the unhappy run-in with his ex, and he couldn't wait to get out of here, away from all the outside pressures he hadn't considered when making the plans for today.

His hands curved around the carryout bags. "I have our food if you're ready."

She chewed her bottom lip, then released it to say, "Uh, thank you."

As he backed into the door, holding it open for her with his body, he decided to go ahead and address the elephant in the room, clear it away so they could move on with the rest of their evening. "An old friend of mine said she ran into you a moment ago. Did she say something to upset you?"

Only a brief wince gave away her discomfort. "I assume you mean Nora. She was perfectly polite." Gabby tightened the belt on her jacket, then turned toward Bella to zip her jacket against the cooling spring evening. "In fact, she was nicer than I would have expected, given she's your girlfriend."

"Former girlfriend," he reminded her.

"Are you seeing someone else?" Gabby asked, pulling a hat for Bella out of the child's monogrammed backpack.

A valid question, and one he should have addressed earlier. "Don't you think my life is complicated enough right now? Trust me, there's no room left for a relationship."

"Right now." She hitched the backpack onto one shoulder while Bella hung on to the hem of her mom's jacket. "Although that's something we'll need to discuss later because anyone in your life affects Bella. But that's a subject for another day. I think my daughter is done for the day."

Her daughter?

Ryan battled the urge to argue with her. Bella was his daughter, too. *Their* child. And he wasn't a man to walk out on his responsibilities. Later, he would think about why that little girl was already starting to feel far more than a responsibility. "I'll bring the car around."

He needed a moment to regroup. Outside, he drew in a deep breath of mountain-fresh night air. The sun had set, the temperature dropping along with it. Streetlamps glowed in the parking lot. A brisk wind swirled in off the valley. The crisp kind of breeze that carried the first hints of spring's promise.

"Son?" his father's voice barked from behind him. "Ryan?"

His father. For real? Karma was kicking his butt today.

Ryan pivoted slowly and sure enough, there stood Thaddeus Taylor, the last person he wanted to see right now. But there was no running away. Bad luck had landed his father here at the same restaurant, heading in just as he was leaving.

"Good evening, Dad." Ryan wished he'd chosen somewhere outside town rather than focusing on showing Gabby all the perks of staying in Bronco as a Taylor. "Where's Mom?"

"At home." His father eyed him intently. "I didn't expect to see you here. I thought you were sick."

"Why would you assume that?" And why had he bothered asking? He should just be shuffling his dad on his way before he noticed Bella and Gabby on the walkway behind him.

In the background, he could hear Bella's tone shift to a higher pitch. Not whiny, just tired. Hungry, too, probably. He really did need to bring the car around.

"You weren't at work today," his dad said slowly, as if irritated over explaining the obvious. "You never take a personal day."

True enough. But these weren't regular circumstances. And Bella's voice grew louder, sounding more agitated. "Well, I did today. Talk to you later. Have a nice dinner."

Gabby was right about how risky today had been bumping into so many people. But he hadn't considered he might come across his father. His dad was supposed to be away on an overnight business trip. At least that's what his mom had said.

Except that must have been an excuse his father gave to cover spending time away from her. Some things never changed.

Gabby tapped him on the shoulder, suddenly closer. "Ryan, Bella and I are ready to go now."

His dad straightened in surprise, almost managing to hide his scowl. "Who's this?"

Ryan froze. Beside him, he sensed Gabby's spine snapping straighter. He wasn't often at a loss for words but right now… He had nothing. This was too important of a moment to risk springing the news about Bella on his father in a parking lot. That wasn't fair to any of them. Might as well let his father think he was on a date. That was safer for the moment.

Bella stepped up alongside him and slipped her tiny hand in Ryan's. His heart squeezed with emotion. Was there a chance his dad would somehow be happy about the news—once the time was right to share? After all, his dad had been hammering him to get married and carry on the family line. While Ryan didn't care what his father thought about his life or decisions, not having to battle Thaddeus Taylor would sure make things easier with Gabby.

Ryan nodded toward the toddler and put his other hand on Gabby's shoulder. "Dad, this is Bella and her mother, Gabrielle Hammond."

The mother of my child. The thought whispered

through his mind as he thought about how all future introductions would proceed.

Thaddeus's forehead furrowed and he smoothed a hand down his tie, tucking it more securely into his suit coat. "Gabrielle, with the veterinary supply company? You just moved to town from the Nashville office, if I'm not mistaken."

"Yes, sir," she answered softly, her hand clenching and unclenching around the backpack strap over her shoulder.

Ryan was surprised his father had taken notice of that. But then his dad was a detail man about business—like keeping track of Ryan's itinerary as if he was still an intern.

His dad thrust his hands into his pockets and rocked back on his heels. "Hello, I'm Thaddeus Taylor, Ryan's father."

Gabby's throat moved in a long swallow. Nerves? "It's nice to meet you."

Bella looked up shyly. "Me gotta book."

The sweet words caught Ryan off guard and under different circumstances might have made him laugh. His father wasn't the bedtime-story sort. In fact, he couldn't recall a single time his father had even tucked him in. Thaddeus had often said that was "women's work."

Ryan searched for the right words to protect Bella from rejection.

Luckily, Gabby leaned down to whisper, "Your

new storybooks are in the car, sweetie. Maybe another time."

The odds of his dad ever being interested in a kid's book were pretty low.

Kneeling, his father pulled a tight smile. "What pretty blue eyes you have, little one. In fact, they look just like my son's."

Gabby's face went sheet white and Ryan suspected his probably looked much the same because all the blood in his body was pounding in his chest. Without thinking, he scooped Bella up and tucked her protectively against him.

Because somehow, his dad figured out the truth and in spite of the smile on his face, the old man didn't look one bit pleased about becoming a grandfather.

Chapter Seven

Gabby hated tension. She'd known that revealing Bella's paternity to Ryan would be tough. But she hadn't fully grasped all the ripples out into this interconnected town. From the scowl on Ryan's face—and total silence as he drove them back to the apartment—the ripples of their complicated relationship had begun to hit him, as well.

Because of his father?

Or did his mood have more to do with the dustup with Nora? Could there be more to that relationship than he'd indicated? Was he still hung up on her?

Better—and safer—to begin with asking about his father. "Your dad was rather, uh…brusque."

At least Bella had drifted off in her car seat, the

last quarter of her quesadilla still clutched in her hand and her new books scattered around her.

Turning the steering wheel with his palm, Ryan entered the parking lot for Gabby's building. The halogen glow of lampposts showcased her minivan, boxed in by the jacked-up truck and the poorly parked sports car.

But dinged door panels were low on her list of worries right now.

His jaw flexed in the orange glow of the dashboard lights. "I would have said he's rude. But your word is certainly more diplomatic." He shot a glance her way, his eyebrows pinching together. "I'm sorry for his behavior outside the restaurant."

"There's no apology necessary." So his anger was directed at embarrassment over his father? Sympathy swept away her frustration. "You're not responsible for how your dad acts."

He tucked the SUV into a guest spot, shifted into Park and pivoted to face her. "For what it's worth, I'm not sure he would have been much nicer to anyone, especially not a female with me. He's on my case to propose to Nora and it's not going to happen."

"The trust issues." And yes, her heart did a leap over hearing him affirm he and Nora were finished. He seemed sincere.

"Hey, I'm also sorry about whatever Nora said or did. It's clear she upset you, and I feel bad for not giving you a heads-up. She's not a bad person." His cheeks puffed with an exhale as he sank back in the seat. "She just expected more from me than I was able to give, even though I'd been very up-front with her. I hurt her."

"Well, I know how that feels," she said tightly, looking away. The last thing she'd expected was to feel sorry for the snooty socialite.

He whistled softly. "So we're back to the missing letters and social media messages again? I don't want to argue with you, especially in front of Bella."

Was he actually correcting her on how to behave around the child she'd been parenting solo for nearly two years because of those missing letters and social media posts? She bristled. "Thank you for the parenting advice. Thank you for the help today. Bella's asleep so there's no need to eat together."

She reached for the door handle. Sure, she was on edge after an emotional day, but that was all the more reason to put some distance between them. ASAP.

"Well, I guess that means I'm not getting a kiss good-night."

His dry humor stopped her short. She wanted to be mad. But his self-deprecating grin reminded her of the appealing nuances to this man's character.

She didn't know whether to laugh or cry. "I think we tried to pack too much into one day so it's for the best that I get Bella straight into her bed, because trust me, a meltdown is only a whisper away when she's tired. Today is too important in your relationship with her. Let's not let her end it on a negative note."

"Everything is more complicated with a toddler in tow, but I enjoyed it." Angled toward her, his broad shoulders blocked out everything else. "And I hope you know how I respect you as a parent. You've done an amazing job with Bella and I welcome your guidance in navigating building a relationship with my daughter."

The tension in her shoulders eased a bit.

"Thank you, I hope you really mean that." How ironic to realize after all the talk about his problems with trust issues, now she had reservations about trusting him.

"Since we're ending this day on a positive note, let me walk you to your door. You can carry Bella so she doesn't wake up and can go straight to sleep. I'll bring the packages and go no farther than your front door. You'll be safely inside with your empanadas and stuffed mushrooms all the faster."

"We're okay. I promise."

"I don't feel comfortable dropping you off alone in the dark."

Even though she was tired, frustrated and hungry, it would be petty not to take him up on the offer. And yeah, he was right. Walking all the way up to the door herself, with Bella and bags, would be a challenge.

"Thank you. I don't mean to sound ungrateful. This is all just…"

"A lot. Yes. Same here." His gaze met hers. "But I'd really appreciate any chance to participate in Bella's life, even if tonight that means helping you get her into her bed so she gets a good night's sleep." His magnetic blue eyes immobilized her.

Stirred her.

Likely because of his reference to a front-door kiss, which stoked memories of so much more than a kiss. That weeklong fling with Ryan had been the most memorable of her life, with a chemistry she'd never experienced before.

All the more reason for her to do everything possible to get into the apartment as soon as possible. Alone.

Ryan wanted to end this day just as much as Gabby had.

But finding his father waiting for him on the front porch of Ryan's home signaled sleep was a long way off. His dad had parked himself in one of the fat rockers lining either side of the door. Ryan would have preferred to put off this conversation until tomorrow, after a decent night's sleep.

That wasn't going to happen anytime soon. His father was an immovable force, a plus in the business world, a negative in the personal realm.

Ryan stopped his vehicle on the circular drive in

front of his home, rather than sweeping around to the garage. Better to keep his father outside. Ryan wasn't a novice in power plays.

He turned off the ignition and stepped out into the night air, wind pushing hard through the mountain pass. "Dad, it's past my bedtime. Can we make this quick?"

His father filled the chair, his Stetson on his knee. "Do you want to tell me what that was all about at The Library with the woman and her child?"

Ryan climbed the wooden steps, his boots thudding. He stopped at the porch post and leaned. Sitting would signal settling in for a long chat. "When I have something to tell you, I will."

"It doesn't work that way," Thaddeus barked in the same tone he'd used Ryan's entire life—from the time Ryan broke a train set as a kid to the day he'd told his father he wasn't going to his alma mater. "Is that your child?"

Sighing, Ryan stuffed his hands into his jeans pockets. "This isn't the way I planned to tell you, but yes. Bella is my daughter."

"How can you be sure?"

Ryan couldn't fault his dad on that question, not when Ryan had asked the same. "The DNA test was conclusive. And before you say anything, I arranged everything through my personal physician."

"All right, then." His father tipped the rocker in motion, the anger all but steaming off him. "How could you have been so stupid as to let this woman trap you for your wealth?"

Ryan didn't consider himself a violent man, but right now, he wanted to slug his father. For the insult to Gabby. For the insinuation that Ryan was gullible. And for all the times that Thaddeus Taylor had disrespected his own wife—Ryan's mother.

"Dad," he said, forcing his voice to stay steady, calm and, most of all, firm, "first of all, who I sleep with is none of your business. And second, I have a real issue with the way you're referring to Gabby. If what you're hinting at was even remotely true, then why would she have waited so long to get in touch with me?"

"So she didn't even bother to tell you she was carrying your child?" His father scowled with disapproval, cupping his Stetson and tapping it against his thigh in an angry tic.

While Ryan still carried anger over that point, his dad couldn't have it both ways. "Now you're mad she didn't tell me sooner when just a second ago you thought it would have been some kind of trick to tell me right away. Dad, you're not making sense."

"I just don't want you to throw away your future on some little gold digger and her illegitimate brat."

That was too far. Ryan straightened and stared his father down. "That is my child and her mother that you're referring to. You would do well to guard your tongue."

His father raised his hands in surrender, hat still

gripped. No doubt a false flag. "Tempers are flaring. Let's think logically. How much do you believe it will take to convince her to leave?"

Everything in Ryan went still—except his pulse, which was roaring in his ears. "Run that by me again?"

"How much money will it take to persuade her never to contact you again?" his dad articulated slowly, as if speaking to a child. "To be clear, I'm willing to write the check. Whatever it takes to get her and that brat of hers to leave town. Oh, and I'll want her to sign papers stating that in accepting the money, she and her child will make no future claim on the Taylor estate. We don't need the stain of illegitimacy on our family name."

"Get off my porch." Ryan stormed past his dad and disarmed his security system.

Thaddeus grabbed Ryan's arm, but his concerned smile wasn't convincing anyone. "I'm just watching out for your best interests."

Ryan stared down at his father. Some part of him still longed for his dad to have a shred of paternal caring inside him. "Don't you want to know your grandchild?" But the answer was written on Thaddeus's face. Ryan shook his head, weary. "Never mind. Don't even bother answering that question. You can take your bribe and stick it."

Ryan stepped into his home, the one he'd built,

not the sterile place where he'd grown up, and he slammed the front door in his pompous father's face.

Their father was a toxic force, especially when it came to women. And Ryan intended to do everything in his power to protect the two most important women in his life—Gabby and Bella.

And even though his father's plan to offer Gabby money to leave town would never work, his dad's concerns over the family name gave Ryan an intriguing idea.

Gabby should have been ready to fall asleep now that Bella was tucked in and she'd polished off the amazing carryout order from The Library. But now, she was wide awake, full of nervous energy.

In the span of the last hour, she'd changed into pj shorts, folded a basket of laundry, fed Elsie, written a polite note to the sports car guy about his parking, then tore it up, wrote a not-nice note, and shredded that one, too, recognizing she was directing her pent-up anger—and hurt—at the wrong source.

Maybe she should bake brownies.

She whipped open the cabinets and started pulling out sealed containers of flour, sugar and cocoa. As she pivoted toward the refrigerator, her cell phone chimed. Her heart sped at the prospect that it might be Ryan. How could she want and dread a call so much at the same time?

A carton of eggs in hand, she leaned to check the

call. From Rylee. Thank goodness, she could use the lift of a fun girl chat. "Hey, friend, glad you called. I'm baking brownies and the house is quiet."

Even Elsie was asleep, curled up in her plaid dog bed a few feet away.

"What in the world happened on your date today?" Rylee's voice was squeaky high with excitement.

"It wasn't a date, and what do you mean?" She put the phone on speaker, then set down the eggs and reached for a stick of butter, placing it on the granite countertop. Then added a second stick to make frosting.

It was a frosting kind of day.

"Everyone is talking about it, Gabby—and by everyone," Rylee said dramatically, "I mean that there are texts flying and even some posts on social media."

"On social media?" She felt like a parrot. These brownies deserved—*she* deserved—extra chocolate chips.

"Yes, along with old photos of him and Nora. Plus some of Nora's friends are commenting, saying things like how they feel sorry for her and how Ryan lost out in losing her." She paused to take a breath. "Keep in mind, I'm just repeating what was said. I do *not* agree at all."

"Okay, slow down and back up." It was a lot to wrap her brain around. She might well need *two* notebooks to keep everything straight. "Besides the Nora Fan Club crowd, what's being said?"

"It all started with pretty benign stuff," Rylee explained. "Someone who cleans stalls at Happy Hearts mentioned seeing the three of you today. Then a volunteer at the Tenacity Animal Shelter chimed in about your visit there, as well. Then, well, there was the bookstore. That's when things started to explode."

Closing her eyes, Gabby sagged back against the counter. How close was this town? "Explode how?"

"Robin Abernathy came to your defense and said Ryan was just showing you around town since you're old friends. Yay, Robin," Rylee cheered. "But also booooo, Robin. You know as well as I do that the best way to fuel a rumor is to give it oxygen. Robin's comment fed that flame a whole bunch of air."

Thinking of all that gossip made Gabby more than a little sick to her stomach. And once they heard the real story, the tongues would really start wagging. "Do they all feel sorry for Nora, too?"

Gabby was a newcomer here after all, unlike Nora.

"Don't worry," Rylee rushed to reassure her. "You may not have been around long, but you're well liked and Bella is adorable. Someone even noted how she's one of the best-behaved little ones in Tender Years Daycare."

That warmed her heart. Bella really was a blessing. Precocious and chatty, but with a caring spirit and the best laugh. "Okay, all that's not so bad."

Her nerves steadying, she started measuring out

the dry ingredients into a bowl while the eggs and butter came to room temperature.

"Then someone mentioned Winona on a walk with Stanley at the park."

"Uh-oh." Though she was a sweet little old lady, Winona was also quirky and reputed to be very chatty.

"Uh-oh is right. Winona may be getting up there in years, but she's still a romantic at heart—rumor is she and Stanley Sanchez may be finally setting a date. Anyhow, back in the day she had a syndicated gossip column called 'Wisdom by Winona.'" Rylee paused for what sounded like a drink through a straw. Her throat must be dry after all the rambling. "So that had antennae on alert...which is when Randall and Mimi John went to—"

"The Library." And there was the nexus of the cloud of gossip. Forget waiting around for room-temp ingredients. She grabbed a second bowl and started cracking eggs.

"Exactly. Mimi overheard some exchange you had with Nora, and then they saw Thaddeus Taylor waylay you on the sidewalk. What happened?"

"Nora warned me that I'm too poor to swim in the Taylor pool and Thaddeus looked down his nose at me." She whipped the whisk through the eggs, slapping the sides of the mixing bowl.

How foolish she'd been to wander around town with Ryan today. This was not the way she'd envisioned revealing Bella's parentage to the world. "None of it was surprising. If it was just about me, I wouldn't be bothered. But I can't bear the thought that someone would make my child feel anything other than totally loved and accepted."

"Oh, my friend," Rylee said, her affection for Bella ringing through, "I one hundred percent agree. I can tell you this. From everything I've noted about Ryan Taylor, he is not like his father. He's a straight shooter. And now that he's accepted Bella as his child, he will move heaven and earth to keep her safe."

Gabby set aside the whisk and starting slicing the butter into the bowl, one plop at a time. "I appreciate the words of support, truly. I treasure our friendship and was really starting to love this town. But now, I'm beginning to wonder if I made the right decision to move to Bronco."

"Hang in there. I'm sure things will smooth over with time." She laughed softly. "And to be fair, you and Ryan didn't help matters by going all over the county together in single day."

"Maybe so, but I also don't think I should have to hide out to avoid being a subject of public interest." They would need to plan their next steps with more caution so Bella was welcomed with love—and not whispers.

Rylee's straw-slurp sounded again before she continued, "How did the day go otherwise? All gossip aside."

Almost perfect, except for the run-ins with Nora and Thaddeus. In fact, the experience would have been pretty perfect if they'd been outside of gossip central. "We had a really lovely time delivering supplies, and his help was incredible. And at the bookstore, he was so sweet and patient with Bella. I couldn't stop my heart from melting a little."

"Aw, I'm so glad he's doing well with her. It's no secret I adore that kid. She gives me baby fever something fierce. If I don't have a kid by thirty, I may very well take my old friend Shep Dalton up on the offer to marry if we're both still single by thirty," she said with a laugh. "But back to you and your day. Tell me more. I. Need. Details!"

The day scrolled through her mind, with flashes of Ryan's smile when Bella took his hand, of their trio of laughter when playing with the puppies. It had been simple. Magical. "And then... Well, we were late getting to The Library and they gave away our reservation. So we decided to get carryout instead." The point where the day soured. "That's when I got waylaid by Nora, then Ryan's dad. It was awkward more than anything—"

"Wait," Rylee interrupted, "so you got carryout? Is Ryan there with you now? Listening?"

"I would tell you if he were here." Honesty was everything. "He left a couple of hours ago. We decided it was best to end the day."

Before she could continue, the doorbell chimed.

"Hey, someone's here. I need to get it before the noise wakes up Bella. Thanks for the heads-up. Love you, friend."

Gabby disconnected the call and dusted her hands on her sleep shorts. Elsie's ears perked up as she went on alert in her dog bed. "Shh," Gabby warned. "Quiet, Elsie."

Padding to the front door, she checked the peephole and found… Ryan? What in the world was he doing back here? She thought they'd agreed to give each other space tonight. Irritation nipped at her insides, but she stifled the urge to snap. The sooner she sent him on his way, the sooner she could return to baking her brownies.

She unlocked and whipped open the door, steeling herself not to notice how handsome he looked in the moonlight. "Did you forget something? I didn't see your wallet or anything in Bella's bag."

"Actually," he said, sweeping off his Stetson and pressing it against his heart, "I did leave something here. I left my family. Marry me."

Chapter Eight

Ryan had never been so sure of anything in his life. Proposing to Gabby so that Bella would have his name made complete sense on many levels. Although based on the look of horror on Gabby's face, he suspected she would need a hefty dose of persuasion.

She grabbed him by the sleeve of his jacket and hauled him into her apartment. "Get in here before someone hears you and lights up the town with even more gossip."

"Let them talk." His chin jutted as he looked around at the other apartment doors. "I would proudly tell the world about my beautiful bride-to-be and our perfect daughter."

Gabby paced away from him, her hands on her shapely hips, her long legs bare in the plaid sleep shorts. He hadn't allowed himself to think much about their shared past while all of his thoughts had been on processing the news of his daughter. But now? Why not enjoy the things that had been so appealing about Gabby in the first place?

She pivoted to face him again, her face full of accusation. "I can't believe you asked me to marry you. Have you been drinking?"

"I'm sober as a judge," he insisted, a bit insulted but determined to keep his cool. Too much rode on him winning this negotiation. "And yes, I asked you to be my wife. I had hoped for a different response."

"I'm not sure I understand where you got that impression." She charged away. "You might as well follow me and explain. I have to finish these brownies before the ingredients spoil."

He worked to keep his eyes off the sway of her bottom and focus on her words. "What do you mean by *more* gossip? Who's been talking?" Was his father already creating trouble? His dad was spiteful, no question, but this didn't seem quite his style.

"Apparently people all over the county have been texting each other about Ryan-Gabby-Bella sightings and theorizing. Your ex-girlfriend Nora didn't help matters."

"Nora's been talking? When? After we left the restaurant?" He was deeply confused. Or maybe his head was still reeling from the massive rejection of his very first marriage proposal.

His father and Nora had been pressuring him to commit, but Gabby seemed determined to keep him at arm's length.

"Not exactly. Someone overheard our conversation. I guess from now on, I'll need to check for feet under all the bathroom stall doors to make sure no one is eavesdropping."

He didn't even have to know who'd been listening. In Bronco, there were dozens of people who would have been riveted. And the mental image of any one of those people hiding out in a bathroom stall, trapped and unable to leave without interrupting the showdown between Nora and Gabby... A much-needed laugh swelled inside him, a relief after a stressful evening.

Gabby dumped sugar into a bowl of butter and eggs with so much force it caused a splash. "It's not funny."

"The speed with which rumors spread around this town is absurd, sure, but also laughable."

She smooshed a spatula through, creaming the sugar, eggs and butter together, adding a splash of vanilla. "Don't forget that Bella was there."

All humor faded from him. "You're right." He leaned back against the counter so he was facing her as she stirred. "What Nora did was totally inappropriate. I'm sorry you were both exposed to that. I'll have words with her—"

"No, please. Just let it go. Talking to her will be

embarrassing and only make it worse. And that's all beside the point. Why are you here and why in the world would you propose?" She began adding small portions of a flour mixture, stirring, then more, stirring again with an overexaggerated precision.

Was she rattled? He needed to tread lightly or she might toss him out. "I proposed for Bella, to give her my name."

"To stem gossip, you mean," she mumbled under her breath, still not meeting his gaze.

"No, of course not. None of that matters to me." He brushed aside her concerns. "You have to admit, though, that it would make things simpler for Bella."

Now that got her attention.

She turned to face him again, pinning him with a pointed stare as she raised an eyebrow. "I don't have to admit anything. If you want Bella to have your surname, we can discuss it, something like a hyphenated Bella Hammond-Taylor. Because to be completely clear, I'm not in the least interested in a loveless marriage of convenience."

Now that was a point he knew exactly how to address.

"Make no mistake," he said, skimming aside her hair, then cupping her shoulder, such a simple touch, but he was caught by surprise how even this much moved him more than anything with another woman. "It won't be a marriage of convenience. Our chemistry was off the charts back in Nashville, and based on the sparks still flying between us, the attraction is still there."

Her pupils widened in awareness, her breath quickening. He angled closer, nearer still until their mouths were a whisper apart. She didn't speak. Neither did he. He watched her eyes, waiting for that precise moment that the tension was strung to a sweet razor's edge and he eased away. She blinked fast, otherwise still.

He crossed his arms over his chest. "But you don't have to answer now. Think about it."

The dazed look faded from her eyes in a snap. "I do *not* need to think about it. Thank you, but no thank you. You can see Bella as much as you would like, but we are not getting married. Do you understand what I'm saying?"

He thought through her rejection, looking for hints on how to persuade her later. The flash of desire in her eyes gave him hope. He'd made progress tonight. He would regroup and come up with a strategy. Bottom line, she hadn't cut him out of Bella's life or threatened to move because of a few busybodies.

"I hear you, including the part about getting to spend time with our daughter. I'll most definitely be taking you up on that. And I'll need your help in learning her routine."

Her eyes narrowed with suspicion. "Are you using Bella to get me to accept your offer?"

Honesty was his best strategy. "I want to spend

time with my daughter. I want to spend time with you."

She sighed in resignation. "There *are* two things we'll need to do right away."

"And what would those be?"

She set aside the bowl and focused her full attention on him. "We need to speak with Bella and find a way to help her understand you're her father—before someone else informs her."

His heart gave an extra thump against his ribs at the prospect. "I would like that. Very much." He swallowed past a lump in his throat before he managed to ask, "What's the second thing?"

"Once we've told the rest of your family about Bella, we need to post a statement on social media to stanch the flow pouring out of the rumor mill. We can craft it tomorrow."

The next day, Gabby warmed her hands in front of the fireplace, plans for pony rides with Bella canceled.

One thing Gabby had learned about Montana weather during her short time in Bronco? Spring was a fickle beast. Some days it was windbreaker weather with the sun shining down on the face. Others? Snow and sleet slung their last salute to winter against the earth.

Today, it was the latter.

She'd already been nervous about spending the day

alone with Ryan—and their daughter—when they were going on a family-style picnic in the great outdoors, but now they were relegated to the entire day at her tiny place. With Ryan currently looking way too handsome in front of her fireplace coaxing a flame to life.

Not unlike the one that still burned inside her after their almost-kiss last night following his outlandish proposal.

As she let the blaze in the hearth warm her, she indulged in a moment to study him, tempted to touch her fingers to the back of his head, his dark blond hair sporting a hint of curl from the damp outdoors.

The day had started off with an inch of snow, so they'd built a miniature snowman with Bella, Elsie prancing around on her leash. Then they'd sledded down the understated hill beside the apartment building.

A bonus to living in a singles complex? Virtually no one was into sliding down an icy hill, as they had no kids. And yes, she'd taken a hint of pleasure out of watching sports car guy spin out in the parking lot before his vehicle disappeared down the road, pumping a cloud of exhaust into the freezing air.

Overall, a simple, easy afternoon.

Then the sleet began, and they'd retreated indoors.

Bella fell asleep for naptime.

Leaving them alone.

Gabby backed away from his tempting body,

curled up in the recliner and wrapped a fleece blanket around her. The wise place to sit. But lonely. She patted her lap for Elsie. The mini-Aussie perked up her head from her dog bed in the corner, looking from Ryan to Gabby, then back to him.

Little traitor.

Again, Gabby tapped her lap. Her pup popped to her feet, trotted over and sprung up to sit with her. For such an explosive energy, Elsie was a lightweight scrap of fur and incredible comfort.

Ryan pressed his hands to his knees and stood, the fire crackling. Did he have to look so mouthwateringly handsome in his well-worn jeans, an open flannel shirt over a dark T-shirt and wool socks? His boots were by the door, alongside hers and their daughter's.

Her heartbeat stumbled. She cleared her throat. "Help yourself to the brownies on the counter. I know lunch was a long while ago."

He laughed softly. "It sure seems like much of our time together lately has revolved around food, but that's a big part of our social gatherings in Bronco."

"The sledding today was fun—and no food involved," she reminded him as he plucked open the container and pulled out a square.

"Bella sure was fearless." Pride radiated from his words and his grin. "I bet we have a future barrel rider there."

"Could be." She skimmed her fingers along Elsie's

silky tri-colored fur. "Would you be okay, though, if she didn't enjoy the ranching life?"

"Of course," he answered without hesitation, his smile fading. "I understand the pressure of a father looking for cookie-cutter kids made in the image of him. My brothers—Daniel and Seth—have a tougher time than I do. As the older ones, they've been the 'heir apparent' for as long as I can remember—alternating in the role depending on which one Dad wasn't mad at that day."

"That must have put a lot of pressure on all three of you boys." She shook her head. "What about your sisters?"

"They walked away—and good for them. Dad is more than a little misogynistic." He put another brownie on a napkin and strode to sit on the floor in front of the hearth—facing her. "He guessed that Bella is my child. He wanted me to pay you off to leave town with her. Because, uh, she doesn't have my name…"

Shrugging, he bit the brownie in half, then chased it with the rest.

Gabby couldn't hold back the gasp. "Are you serious?"

"He thought he could buy your silence." The pain in his deep blue eyes was unmistakable.

"Well, he was wrong there," she snapped.

"And I'm thankful for that." He crumpled the napkin and pitched the wad into the fireplace, the flames devouring the paper. "He still has the misguided notion that I should be with Nora—and that's never going to happen."

Her father may have been absent—a horrible fact—but at least he hadn't been poisoning her life like Ryan's. "Is that why you proposed? Because of what your father said?" She hadn't taken the proposal seriously, but it hurt all the more to think he'd only asked because of pressure from his dad. "You mentioned wanting her to have your name."

He scrubbed a hand along his collarbone as if rubbing away pain. "Trust me, I don't care what he thinks. But him mentioning us not being married made me realize how much sense it made for us to become a couple."

Still not a vow of love—which she didn't want and could hardly expect considering their brief time together—but definitely better to know the proposal had come from Ryan. She still felt a lingering pinch of sympathy over how his father had treated him, rejecting his own flesh and blood.

"Thank you for the fire," she said. "It brings back happy memories. On days like this, Mom and I used to light the fire in the fireplace, make hot chocolate and put together a jigsaw puzzle. I know that may sound simple to a guy like you."

He tipped his head, shadows playing along the hard planes of this face. One long leg was stretched in front of him, the other bent, his arm resting on his knee. "What do you mean 'a guy like me'?"

"Isn't it obvious?" She motioned toward the whole look of him, his wealth and power emanating even when his feet sported nothing more than winter wool socks. And did he realize how close his outstretched leg was to her? "You can afford entertainment a lot more expensive than a puzzle. You can jet wherever you like, see any show, eat at any restaurant. Besides, a rodeo seems more your speed for excitement."

"Yes," he conceded, shifting, his foot bumping lightly against her ankle. "I can afford the things you listed and yes, I live for a rodeo, but that doesn't mean I can't enjoy the simple things in life."

"Such as puzzles?" She couldn't quite envision him parked at a card table working a thousand-piece puzzle of the Grand Canyon.

He chuckled, stroking his toes along the arch of her foot. "Not puzzles, exactly. More like sleeping by the campfire after cooking my dinner over the open flame. Fly-fishing in one of our streams. Walking the land after the first big blizzard and hearing the snow crackle with each step."

The image he painted with his words was vibrant, enticing. And curious. "If you love being outdoors so much, why are you working in an office?"

She gulped down the tingles of awareness at his touch through her cotton socks, bringing memories of their fling. Of the time they'd sat facing each other in the overlarge spa tub. Now he clasped her foot, massaging it. Her toes curled. An arch of his brow gave the only indication that he'd noticed.

But he didn't stop. "I work the corporate side because it's necessary to hold on to the land. And we hold on to that land because riding, walking, camping and everything else that's good in life don't hold nearly as much appeal unless I'm doing them on *our* property."

His love of the family legacy was undeniable. So tangible in fact, she couldn't escape a deeper truth. No matter how deeply his dad hurt him, regardless of what jerk moves his father pulled next, the Triple T was built on a family fabric, all of them woven together, the good and the bad.

By bringing Bella into Ryan's world, her child was now a part of that complicated dynamic. Gabby would need to keep all her wits about her to look out for her daughter, to make sure Bella stayed grounded in the simpler joys and values of life.

And if a simple toe caress to the arch of her foot set Gabby's insides into this much turmoil, anything more was most definitely out of the question.

Ryan wondered why he hadn't thought of suggesting a day like this at the start, hanging out together away from the pressures of living in the fish-bowl town of Bronco. And he intended to make the most of this afternoon with Bella and Gabby, an afternoon that was stretching into an evening.

Sleet coated the roads, and even though he could have made his way safely home, the weather conditions offered a decent excuse to stay here longer.

He'd been inspired by the conversation with Gabby about the great outdoors. So when Bella woke from her nap, he'd enlisted her help to build a blanket fort with a pile of pillows in front. The power kept flickering off and on, so keeping the roaring fire going seemed wise.

And staying to look after Gabby and Bella seemed even wiser.

Gabby sat cross-legged on the floor, French braiding Bella's hair to match hers while he fed another log into the blaze. Taking in the sight of the two of them would be too easy.

He jabbed the poker into the stacked wood, releasing sparks up into the chimney. "When I was a little boy, I camped outside a lot."

Bella's eyes went wide—Taylor blue eyes. "Outside?"

"Yes, ma'am, I sure did," he said, the memories some of his favorites from growing up, "with my brothers and my sisters. We rode our horses—we had grown-ups with us, too. Because going alone would be unwise."

"Like Mommy?" she asked earnestly.

He searched for a diplomatic way to explain his

parents' absence. Not easy and he wasn't even sure how much she would understand. But he'd noticed that Gabby didn't use baby talk around their daughter and so he followed her example. "Uh, not my mother. My brothers were older. And we had other grown-ups." The foreman and stable manager. In hindsight, it was a lot like how the nanny put them to bed at home. "When we camped out, we cooked over the fire."

Her gaze shot to the hearth, then back to him as she leaned forward to listen. "Cookin'?"

Gabby steadied her from scooting too far away as she continued to weave the strands of whispery hair together. She'd been quiet since their talk earlier and he wondered why. But now wasn't the time to ask. Right now, his focus was on bonding with Bella.

"Hot dogs," Ryan listed, ticking off the list on his fingers, "popcorn, bacon, burgers. But my favorite was a grilled peanut butter and jelly sandwich."

Giggling, Bella clapped her hand over her mouth. "Silly."

"Nope," he said with exaggerated sincerity, "it's very yummy. Would you like to try it for supper? We can cook it for your mom."

"Mommy." She tipped her head back to plead, looking too cute in her pink floral sweat suit. "Pwease?"

Ryan had a momentary panicked thought. "Bella's not allergic to peanuts, is she?"

"Thank goodness, no. Peanut butter is a big staple

in her diet." Gabby twisted a rubber band around the end of Bella's braid, then kissed her daughter on top of her head. "Strawberry jelly is her favorite."

Gabby's ease with her child, the love shown in even the simplest of tasks, tugged at him. He hadn't known he was choosing a mother for his child when he'd initiated the fling with Gabby, but he was eternally thankful for Gabby's nurturing presence in Bella's life.

"All right, then." Ryan clapped his hands against his knees, standing. "Three grilled PBJ sandwiches coming up."

In fast order, he dug out the cast-iron skillet he'd seen earlier, then gathered up a loaf of bread, peanut butter, jelly and butter.

He deposited all the makings on the hearth under the watchful eyes of the two females. "Ladies, get ready for some campfire cooking."

Gabby rose to her knees. "Can I help?"

"No, ma'am. Don't mess with the chef." He made fast work of slathering the ingredients inside one, two, three sandwiches while the pan heated over the fire. Once the two tablespoons of butter melted, he placed each PBJ inside to begin browning. The aroma of childhood memories wafted up in a strawberry-buttery blend before he turned to face Gabby. "What was your favorite food as a kid?"

"Grilled cheese." A smile lit her brown eyes. "With two slices of cheddar."

"How about we make that during the next black-out family dinner?"

Gabby went still at the word *family*. She licked her lips nervously, which then made him freeze, too. How did other parents deal with frustrating chemistry when little ones were hours away from bedtime? He focused on flipping the PBJs in the skillet.

"Family," Gabby whispered, her shoulders bracing. "All right, I think it's time to tell Bella."

His scrambled brain worked to untangle what she meant only to finally understand. She was ready to tell their daughter about him being her father.

His gut clenched. He wanted this, sure, but now that the moment had come, he felt far from ready with little to no background to draw upon for how to handle something this monumental with a child. "You should be the one to say it." He set aside the pan onto the hearth, out of the flame, because no doubt, he would burn the sandwiches to a crisp otherwise. "You'll know the right words to help her understand."

Relief flooded her face. "Thank you. I appreciate that." Gabby's hand gravitated to Elsie, stroking, as she turned to her daughter. "Bella, sweetie, before we start eating, we need to talk to you for a minute."

"Okey dokey." She plopped on her bottom, her cheeks still red from windburn in the cold earlier.

Gabby drew her pup closer. A sign of stress? "Did you have fun yesterday?"

"I wuv pigs and puppies." Bella hugged her knees.

"And we love spending time with you." Gabby's voice was soothing, loving, so calm no one would have guessed she was rolling out such a monumental revelation. "It was nice having Mr. Ryan with us."

She nodded fast, the tail of her braid bobbing. "I got this many books." She tried to hold up her fingers, but her face scrunched as she worked to get it right. "Lots of books. Tank you."

"And he pushed you on the swing, too," Gabby continued.

Bella rocked backward on her bottom, squealing.

Gabby smoothed her daughter's bangs from her forehead. "You're such a sweet girl. Would you like for Ryan to come to the park with us always?"

Squealing, Bella popped to her feet, dancing in a circle. "Yes, yes, yes!" Elsie sprang into action joining the jig. "Mine fwiend?"

"Yes, he's our friend." Gabby waited for the twirling to slow, then eased Bella into her lap. Elsie sat, her wagging tail sweeping the carpet. "But he's also more than a friend. He's also *family*."

Bella's forehead scrunched in confusion. "Huh?"

Gabby continued to hold her daughter lightly. Securely. Then she leaned closer and explained, "Mr. Ryan is your daddy."

"Mine dada?" Her blue eyes shifted to him.

Looking for confirmation?

Ryan's throat closed up so he just nodded. He held his breath. Bella's reaction would mark the most important moment of his life. Thank goodness he didn't have to wait long.

"Yay," she cheered, then tipped her head to the side. "Eat now, Dada?"

His gaze met Gabby's over their daughter's head, her eyes full of emotion and even a sheen of tears. He mouthed the words *thank you* before returning his attention to Bella. In that simple moment, his whole world shifted. Her sweet acceptance was more than he could have hoped for, and more than he deserved. But he was thankful to the depths of his soul.

"Yes, baby girl. We can have the sandwiches now." And as he led her over to the counter, his heart in her hands, he knew he would do anything for his daughter.

Chapter Nine

Having someone help her with Bella's bedtime routine was a bittersweet mixture of good and alien. Now that their daughter had been tucked in with four bedtime stories—Gabby and Ryan alternated—she eased the door closed, too aware of the solitude. Except that child-free alone-time wasn't solitary tonight.

Ryan's broad shoulders now filled her corridor and fantasies.

What would happen next? Would he go? Should she invite him to stay? One thing was for certain. They needed to move back into the living room so as not to wake up Bella.

She raised a finger to her lips, then motioned for him to follow her. His hand rested lightly on her waist. Gulp.

Nerves skittered up and down her spine, chasing the goose bumps launched by his touch. What next?

Once they'd reached the family room, he drew up alongside her. "What do you say I take Elsie out for a bathroom break for you before I leave?"

So he wasn't going to press for more from her today. She didn't know whether to be relieved or disappointed. Maybe she wanted to be the one to say no. For her pride? Regardless, he was being considerate. She needed to meet him halfway.

"I appreciate the offer. How about I go with you? We can stick close to the patch of grass near my front door and I'll bring the baby monitor."

His smile was a heady reward.

Five minutes later, she sat on the front stoop, cradling the baby monitor while Ryan held the long leash and allowed Elsie to sniff to her heart's content. The lot was mostly quiet in that sweet spot of time when the singles were either out partying or in their apartments with friends. Folks around here didn't call it a night at eight in the evening.

Gabby hugged her jacket tighter around her, tugging it so the hem was securely under her bottom to keep from freezing her tush on the cold concrete. At least the snow and sleet had stopped, the air carrying that fresh-washed scent.

Like her life.

Today, telling Bella about her father, marked a new chapter in the little girl's life. Going forward, this date would mark the line between the before and after.

Ryan must feel the magnitude of that as well, not that he was letting on. "Are you okay? How did you feel about the way I related the news to Bella about you being her father?"

"You handled it masterfully. I'm thankful," he said with sincerity.

But his answer lacked specificity.

"You didn't address my other question. How are *you*?"

He lowered his gaze, watching Elsie with an exaggerated concentration as if needing to dig deep to find a response. Did he make a habit of hiding his feelings?

Kneeling to scratch the dog behind the ears, he finally said, "I expected to be moved. But I had no idea."

He tapped himself over his flannel-covered heart, his jacket open and loose. The understatement spoke louder than a speech. And yes, she understood what he meant. Completely.

"Parenthood is an incredible honor." She remembered the wonder of the day she gave birth. The overwhelming love. Was he feeling a portion of those emotions now?

The joy in his eyes was muted by shadows, however. She suspected he was thinking of the first two years of Bella's life and all he'd missed.

She stuffed her chilly hands into her coat pockets.

"I'd like to make a deal with you. Let's not debate any longer about the miscommunications after our fling. We focus forward on Bella."

"Agreed," he said, standing and crossing to sit beside her, leash still in hand. His muscular thigh pressed against hers. "We're communicating now and that's what matters."

"It's nice." She bumped her shoulder against his. "I enjoyed our time putting Bella to bed. And thank you for the help with Elsie, too."

"I'm uncomfortable with you being out here alone at night," he said under his breath, as if already knowing she would argue.

"I appreciate your concern." And she did. But she was careful about safety for her and for her child. "There are plenty of security cameras here and everyone's nice. Well, except for sports car guy."

Ryan looked up sharply, scowling. "Sports car guy?"

"It's nothing big or dangerous," she rushed to reassure him. "He has the parking spot next to mine. He says I dinged his car door. But I didn't. He parks too close, so he assumed it was me. When it's too tight like that, I'm careful to exit from the other side of my van. One time, when the truck was in the other spot, I even had to crawl in through the back hatch." She finished with a nervous chuckle, thankful that Bronco social media hadn't latched on to photos of that.

Ryan wasn't laughing. "You said he parks too close? Did you tell him?"

Her smile faded. "He said it's his choice if he wants to be right by the white line as long as he's not over."

"He sounds like a jerk."

"A rich jerk," she said as Elsie trotted over to curl up on top of her feet.

He quirked an eyebrow.

She sighed, her breath a puffy cloud in the cold air. This probably wasn't the best time to tell him that parking lots made her twitchy since her mother had been killed in one, in a freak accident when she'd been hit by a car backing up. Until now, she hadn't really made the connection that her level of irritation at sports car guy could be rooted in missing her mom. "This is a place geared more for young singles. Sometimes I feel like this fella is trying to chase me off because he doesn't like kid noise."

"I'll take care of it." His jaw was tight, testosterone all but oozing from his pores.

"Hold on." She rested a hand on his knee. "I didn't ask you to do that. I absolutely don't want you making use of your last name to influence someone."

"I'm not my father." His shoulders braced defensively. "That's not how I would handle it."

Still, no. "Thank you for the offer, but we're okay."

He rested his hand on top of hers, his palm broad and warm. "You know what would be the simplest solution? Move in with me."

"I already said no." She shook her head, but didn't pull away.

"You said no to a proposal." He linked their fingers, squeezing. "What about sharing a house?"

"No." The word fell out of her mouth hard and fast.

"Okay, I hear you. What about living in a cabin on the property?" He tapped her mouth with a finger. "Wait. Hear me out. It'd be lots of land for Bella and Elsie. Less driving for me to see her. If you have to work late or daycare is closed, I'm nearby. It makes sense."

She hesitated, resisting the urge to lick her lips. "Thank you. But that's a pretty big step."

"I understand things are moving fast. For me, too," he said with a self-deprecating wince. "What do you say we start off with you and Bella spending some time at the ranch, just to let you and her get used to the space and my world? Once I tell my mother and my siblings about Bella, they will want to meet her."

His siblings, his mom? She prayed they weren't like his father. Regardless, they were unavoidable. Bella deserved to know her family. "Of course."

"I'll show you around, let you see the setup with the cabins." His words picked up speed, his enthusiasm for his home shining through. "And if you decide a cabin is in your future, consider it part of child support." She opened her mouth but before she could speak, his finger on her lips once again stalled her. "Just promise me you'll think about it."

It was a lot to process. Still, she nodded, and meant it. She'd planned dozens of times how to tell Ryan about Bella, but she hadn't thought beyond that. Little had she known that would be the easy part. Actually meshing their lives would be far more complicated. At least she had an olive branch to start with while she considered his cabin offer.

"I've selected some photos of Bella from the past couple of years to share with you." She'd stayed up late last night working on it, her heart tight thinking about all he'd missed from her first day of life to her first steps. "The order has been placed. It's a book style, with captions. It'll be ready in another day or two."

"Thank you. That means a lot to me." His throat moved in a slow swallow she was beginning to realize was his "tell" for deep emotions.

She swayed closer, her hand falling to rest on his chest, the warmth of him reaching through his flannel shirt. "We can pick it up when you show me around your ranch."

"Sounds perfect." He skimmed his fingers over her cheek. "Good night, Gabby."

His mouth sketched over hers so briefly, she wondered for a moment if she'd imagined it. Until she looked into his eyes and saw the heat flaring. She touched his lips lightly, tempted to take more. But for Bella's sake, she couldn't risk complicating matters any further. Especially with a man who was already tossing around marriage proposals.

"Good night, Ryan."

A smile kicked up one corner of his mouth. He passed her Elsie's leash, stood and tipped his Stetson in farewell.

As she watched his long-legged strides take him across the parking lot into the crisp night, she knew without question that she hadn't sent him away just to protect Bella.

She was guarding her own heart, as well.

Stepping through the door at Doug's bar, Ryan dragged in a bracing breath of Bronco Valley night air. No doubt about it, he was drained. Usually, a guy-time with friends recharged him, but the evening with his buds at Doug's had been flatter than day-old beer on a day that had already kicked his butt.

Telling his siblings about Bella earlier had put him through the wringer. He'd chosen to share the news about Bella with them by phone before talking to his mother. He'd thought it would be easier to start off with them.

Wrong.

His brothers had reiterated their concerns that he be careful so no one got hurt. His sisters had been thrilled, and protective, concerned about how he would shield Bella from their father's negativity. Their concerns had been justified.

But no doubt about it, Ryan needed a reset before talking to his mother, so he'd accepted Dylan Sanchez's invitation to join him and some friends for drinks.

Ryan had gone through the motions, shooting the breeze with ranchers Shep Dalton and Theo Abernathy. The Burris brothers had shown up in force with tales of their latest rodeo feats. An hour in, Ryan had vacated the red leather barstool and made his way toward the exit.

As the door swung closed and muffled the cacophony of voices, he flipped up the collar of his leather jacket against the evening chill and strode down the sidewalk to the packed parking lot out back. He secured his Stetson and kept his head down, discouraging any passersby from making idle chitchat. Boots crunching gravel, he had to admit to himself that he really just wanted to talk to Gabby, to phone her and hear her voice with those husky tones that turned him inside out.

And he would say…what? He scrubbed a hand along the back of his neck just as a voice shouting his name drew him up short. He glanced back to find Ross Burris and Theo trailing after him. He was surprised to see them leaving early, too, but asking would delay his departure.

Theo pulled out his key fob and pointed it toward his truck. "You look miserable, Ryan. Did you accidentally sit on the haunted barstool and unleash its curse?"

Ryan winced. That was the last thing he needed. Legend had it, a man died on that particular barstool, leaving it cursed, bringing grief to anyone who sat on his fatal seat. "I gave it a wide berth."

Nodding approval, Theo stuffed his keys back in his pocket. "I know we agreed not to talk about women tonight, but you've gotta know that didn't stop the whispers."

Ryan winced. Time was running out before the truth about Bella leaked, which didn't leave him much time to explore his feelings for Gabby without undue scrutiny. Not to mention, he still had to tell his mother. "I'm aware."

"And you're okay dating a woman who already has a kid?" Theo, a dyed-in-the-wool bachelor, lifted a skeptical eyebrow.

Dating? If only it were that simple. "Little Bella is a charmer."

Rodeo royalty Ross Burris drew up behind them. Ross's brothers Jack and Mike were still inside. Ross had always been the charming brother, the one ladies flocked around. "Just the kid, huh? It's no secret that I'm not interested in a committed relationship. The life of a rodeo cowboy doesn't lend itself to settling down. But even I can recognize when a guy's been hooked by a female." He clapped a hand on Ryan's shoulder. "You've been itching to leave this evening since you set foot in the door."

Theo chuckled. "I couldn't have said it better." He stepped back. "All right then, Ryan, we'll ease up on you—for now. Good night."

No one needed to tell him twice. Ryan shot a wave to his buddies. "We'll catch up later."

As Ryan settled behind the wheel of his SUV, the urge to call Gabby hadn't left. But he didn't want to spook her and lose ground by moving too fast.

Better to wait until he saw her in person during the tour of the ranch tomorrow and could gauge her mood by her expressions.

Besides, there was still the matter of informing his mom about her new granddaughter.

Putting the SUV into Drive, he nailed the accelerator, letting the powerful engine eat up the miles quickly back to the Triple T.

Before heading to his place, though, he decided to stop off at his parents' house first to talk with his mother. A brief text exchange with her reassured him she was still awake.

Now, as Ryan stood outside the door to Imogen's suite, he tamped down the turmoil inside him. He needed a cool head to make it through this important moment. It was one thing to have his father's disapproval, but if his mother bailed on his child, as well? Ryan wasn't sure how to come back from that.

He tapped on the door, waiting.

"Come in, dear," his mother called out.

His mother's suite was made up of a sitting room, in addition to her bedroom, dressing room and bath. And separate from his father's suite. When asked why they didn't share a room like other kids' moms and dad, his mother had simply said that her husband snored too loudly. Ryan always wondered though if his mom needed a haven, a place to relax away from Thaddeus's domineering ways.

Was it any wonder he wanted more of a practical arrangement for himself? One with less tension? A partnership? And since he and Gabby already had a child together, spending his life with her was a logical choice. Her down-to-earth nature and their chemistry made the prospect all the sweeter.

But that wasn't what he was here to discuss with his mother.

Imogen had prepared to receive him, dressed in slacks, with a matching sweater set. Did she wear pearls to sleep? He and his siblings had jokingly debated that more than once.

She sat in one of the two wingbacks in front of the fireplace, the end table sporting a plate of fat oatmeal raisin cookies.

"Hello, Mom," he said, dropping a kiss on her upturned cheek. "I have some important news to tell you."

She motioned toward the chair on the opposite

side of the fireplace. "Have a cookie first. I had the cook send up your favorites."

He didn't bother correcting her that she had the wrong kid. His were chocolate chip, or rather that used to be his preferred treat. Now, he had a new appreciation for brownies.

"Thanks, Mom." He plucked one from the plate and chewed through a bite. "About that news—"

"I've already heard from your father," she said, toying with her necklace.

He hadn't expected his father to share the information with Imogen. Thaddeus hadn't said anything to the other siblings. So why? Their dad never did anything without an agenda.

"I'm sorry for not telling you myself." Maybe that had been the agenda—attempt to drive a wedge between mother and son. "Dad and I had a disagreement. I didn't think he would say anything, given how he refuses to acknowledge my child."

"He'll come around." She brushed aside the mammoth concern as if it were nothing more than a disagreement over what restaurant to have dinner in. "He wasn't always entirely thrilled every time I was pregnant, but he is very proud of his children."

That didn't make him feel much better. He popped the other half of the oatmeal raisin cookie into his mouth. "Which one of us was unwanted?"

She nudged the tray of cookies an inch closer, diamond wedding ring set glinting. "I never said *un-wanted*."

She had sure implied as much. But it was clear his mother had gone back into denial, a safer place for her to exist in her marriage. He needed more clarity right now. "To be clear, Bella is very much wanted. She's my daughter and I love her."

"What about her mother?" Imogen's eyes twinkled with interest. "Is she loved, as well?"

Something in him wanted to confide, to have his mother help him wade through this complicated turn in his life, to be a parent he could turn to. Because if she could be that, then perhaps there was hope for him with his child, as well. "I've asked her to marry me, but she turned me down."

"Son, that's not what I asked you." She leaned forward and clasped his hands. "I wanted to know if you love her."

"I did ask her to marry me."

"Love and marriage don't always go hand in hand."

Was his mother hinting at something? She'd always insisted that she loved Thaddeus despite his failings. Ryan just hoped his mom was loved equally in return. He wasn't always too sure of that. "According to Gabby love and marriage should—as you say—go hand in hand."

She gave his hands a final squeeze before letting go. "I like this girl already. Now when do I meet my granddaughter?"

Her easy acceptance was one weight off his shoulders, at least. Even if he was a long way from having family matters settled.

"Bella and Gabby are coming over tomorrow to spend the afternoon."

The twinkle in her eyes multiplied. Joy. His mom was happy. And even if her marriage wasn't everything she'd hoped, she still found obvious delight in her family.

But was that enough to hold a relationship together? Ryan knew better. And the fact that a family bond couldn't replace the emotional connection of romantic love only underscored Gabby's reluctance to move in with him. A fact that didn't bode well for his own future.

Gabby knew about the Triple T in theory, from numbers on a spreadsheet and photos.

None of that could have prepared her for the grand reality.

Holding on to the side of the large ATV—Bella kept calling it a golf cart, which made Ryan laugh— she took in the last of their tour. Bella sat between them, her car seat buckled in tight. Her child's oohs and aahs and nonstop pointing were endearing.

She echoed the sentiments.

Her brain was on overload from the magnificence of the Taylor spread. Like a kaleidoscope of beautiful images. The expanse of rolling pastures leading into the mountains. Barns, a stable and a bunkhouse beyond any she'd seen even in her work selling veterinary supplies.

And the animals. Cattle. Horses. Barn cats and family dogs. This place was the stuff fantasies were made of. And as much as she wanted security for Bella, Gabby felt a loss of control that the people here would have an influence over her child. As much as she wanted to trust Ryan when he said the others weren't like his father, what if…?

She willed her focus back onto the present, her happy child and the ruggedly handsome man behind the wheel. The main house had been overwhelming from the outside. Ryan's home on the property had been less intimidating, but still so huge for one person. She could breathe a little easier when he'd driven by the guest cabins. They'd been charming and reasonably sized. She could almost envision living in one with Bella.

Not that she was ready to make such a big concession yet.

"Your family's property is incredible. So stunning."

The ATV jostled lightly along bumpier ruts in the grass. He stretched an arm along the back of the seat, reaching past Bella to cup Gabby's shoulder. It felt right, special, the three of them as a unit.

"This is Bella's legacy now, too." The wind ruffled his sun-burnished hair. "I've already spoken to my lawyer about setting up a trust fund for her."

His words kicked her worries up a notch. "I wish you would have spoken to me about that first. I don't want Bella to grow up with a silver spoon in her mouth—no offense."

"None taken." He nodded in concession. "Although I can give away money to anyone I choose." He held up a hand. "But I will make a point to try better in the future."

"Thank you." She wanted to trust him.

"Well—" he winced, his forehead furrowing "—starting tomorrow, because today, I already bought a new pony for her to, uh, see."

A pony? He couldn't fool her; she knew he'd bought the pony for Bella. At least he hadn't sprung it on their daughter, which would have made it all but impossible for Gabby to say no. "We can talk more later."

"Gabby, the last thing I want is to do anything to upset you. Can't you see I'm trying my best to get you and Bella to move here?" He slowed the vehicle as they neared the main stables, pulled up to the large barn doors and turned off the ignition.

A female in scuffed boots and a flannel jacket lounged on the split rail fence. "About time you got back here, brother. I was close to freezing my butt off waiting to catch a glimpse."

"Allison," Ryan called out, stepping from behind the wheel, thankful his sister had been able to come home to visit Eloise and her baby Merry, "you could have stayed at the house like I asked and been toasty warm."

Gabby watched the exchange, wary. She'd hoped to wait a little longer before meeting his family. Preferably after she had time to process all she'd seen today.

But telling Ryan about their daughter had been like releasing a giant snowball that rolled downhill, gaining speed and size of its own accord. There was no stopping the momentum now.

Allison hopped from the fence. "What can I say? I'm curious. And I care."

Finished unbuckling Bella, Gabby hefted up her wriggling daughter, only to set her down before she dropped her. Out here, Bella didn't cling or suck her thumb. She took off running toward the fence.

"Whoa." Ryan whistled, scooping her up around the waist. "Slow down there, kiddo. We don't want you getting stomped by a horse now."

He hefted her up onto his shoulders, where she hung on tight, her fingers gripping his hair. "Gabby, Bella, this is my middle sister, Allison."

Allison thrust out a hand. "Welcome. It's a delight to meet you both." She gave Bella a wink and a little plastic pony with a purple silky mane. "And this is for you. It's a magic horse."

Squealing, Bella reached and thank goodness Ryan still held her legs firmly. "Tank you. Pwetty pony."

"You're very welcome." Allison grinned and seemed genuine. "What are you going to name her?"

Bella's face scrunched up for a moment before she said, "Pwetty Pony."

Gabby watched the exchange with a mama bear protectiveness, hoping this family understood that if they intended to charm her daughter, they had better not flake later.

Allison tapped her brother on the arm and waved toward the barn. "Brother, take this adorable little one to see the new pony. I'll keep Gabby occupied."

Ryan shot her a nervous glance. "Allison, stop being transparent—"

Gabby rested a hand on his elbow. She could hold her own. Besides, it would give her a chance to get a real measure of the woman and issue some gentle warnings of her own. "I'm fine. Really. Bella, have fun seeing the pony and behave."

"Yay," Bella cheered. "Giddy-up, Dada."

Hearing her daughter call him that still caught her by surprise, even as happiness bubbled inside her. Things were going so well. Almost too well. There had to be a catch. Her mother had always warned her to be prepared for the unexpected.

Allison tipped her face to the sun, her ponytail streaming down her back. "How mind-blowing to hear my brother called Dada. That's something I never thought would happen."

Well, it hadn't been by choice. "He's good with her."

"So it seems. We sure didn't have much of a role model, though." Allison started walking, leaving

Gabby no choice but to follow. "I don't know how much Ryan has told you, but our dad is tough. It's no secret my sisters and I keep our distance from him."

"Ryan's mentioned it." What was the woman's point with this conversation? Because she was sure diving right into the heavy stuff. No getting-to-know-you chitchat.

"I thought you should be warned in advance, just in case. That's why I came out here uninvited." She paused at the fence again, digging into her pocket for a sugar cube. "To say our father is misogynistic is putting it mildly."

"He's not thrilled about Bella and me, either." Everyone probably already knew that.

A warrior light glinted briefly in the other woman's eyes.

"I'll be putting him on notice. That's my niece." She held out her palm as a quarter horse trotted over to nibble the cube. Allison's jaw flexed before she turned back toward Gabby. "I've known Bella for all of a couple of minutes and already I would take a bullet for her."

It was a strong statement, but Gabby believed her. Allison, at least, would be a protector in this sprawling family of strong personalities.

"Thank you, she's pretty special." Gabby glanced back over her shoulder, hoping to catch sight of them, but no luck. Although her daughter's giggles riding the breeze reassured her that all was well.

"I agree," Allison said, fishing in her pocket for another cube and offering it to Gabby. "I'm glad you and she are in my brother's life."

"Oh, we're not a couple anymore," Gabby rushed to deny while taking the sugar cube so as not to appear rude. "We never were, actually. It was more of a fling. Short term. We went our separate ways. We had a, uh, miscommunication that kept him from learning about Bella. But that's fixed now." She extended her palm, the horse's nibble tickling her skin.

"I'm so glad." Allison leaned closer to run a soothing hand along the mane as it rippled in the wind. "You have to know, though, that Mom's going to spoil her."

Gabby willed away the fresh kick of nerves. The woman was just using generalities. Grandparents spoiled grandkids. No big deal.

Unless the grandparents were gazillionaires.

Before Gabby could scavenge a benign answer, Allison gave the horse a final pat on the neck and backed up a step. "Well, I should let you get back to your tour. I promised Mom that I would help her get things together for the family supper."

Panicked, Gabby froze in her tracks. "Family supper?"

Chapter Ten

"One horse, two horses, three horses," Ryan chanted to Bella as he carried her past the stalls on their way back out of the barn.

Was he being a pushy dad in trying to help her learn to count? Or was this the way he should talk to her? He wasn't used to second-guessing every move he made. But then he'd never been a dad before. The stakes had never been higher. He refused to be a distant, critical father like his own, and made a mental note to find some parenting books for guidance.

Bella recited after him, "One, two, free...four?"

"Yes, Bella-girl, that's great. You're such a smart one."

Her smile made him feel like he'd won the lottery. Pausing, he let her stroke the muzzle of a palomino, impressed with her ease around the animals. Buzz stayed still, even his breaths slowing, acting careful around the child. Ryan had found that most horses had better instincts than people.

Part of why he felt most at home here, with the smell of hay, leather and saddle oil. He preferred the view of tackle-covered plank walls to sleek boardrooms. But the corporate world helped protect the legacy for future generations.

For his daughter.

A rustle behind him drew his attention to Gabby approaching slowly, her boots scuffing tracks on the dirt floor. Her shell-shocked expression set off alarms in his mind.

"Are you okay?" He shifted Bella to his other hip so he could grasp Gabby's shoulder. "Did my sister say something to upset you?"

Blinking clear the dazed look in her brown eyes, she shook her head. "Not at all. She was very welcoming. But what's this about a family dinner?"

"The three of us are spending the day together. Aren't we?" They'd even made arrangements for Rylee to watch Elsie so Gabby could have the whole day free. He passed a carrot to Buzz before stepping away.

"That's not what I mean." She smoothed back wisps of Bella's hair as the child rested her head on Ryan's shoulder. "Your sister said there's a *family* supper."

"I don't know what you're— Oh man. *My mom.*"
He scrubbed a hand along his jaw. He could only
imagine all the hoops his mother must have jumped
through to get everyone here at the same time, no
small feat. "I'm sorry, but she must have planned a
family get-together. I'll just tell her it's too much for
Bella and we'll do it another time."

"No, no, please." She held her hands up in panic.
"I don't want her first impression of me to be one
of rejection. I just wish I'd known so I could have
dressed a little nicer."

"You look great."

And she did. Her beauty was the all-natural kind
that didn't depend on artifice. From her hair piled
loosely on top of her head to her dusty boots.

She swept her hand from her windbreaker to her
faded jeans. "I look like I've been in a barn all day."
As if sensing the tension, the quarter horse just ahead
began pawing the ground, snorting. She pointed to
the chestnut mare. "See, even she agrees."

"If that's the case, then, lady, you make 'barn'
look good," he said with a wink, before easing Bella
to the ground and pulling out his phone to shoot off a
text to his sisters. "We're a casual crew, but if you're
worried, I'm sure one of my sisters will have something you can wear. They still keep clothes here."

Scrunching her nose, she shifted from foot to foot.
"I don't want to put them out."

"Too late." He held up his cell. "Already sent the

message. They'll be thrilled to help. No need to worry. We don't do big, formal meals anyhow. It'll be fine."

Her gaze skated down to Bella, their daughter sitting on the packed earth and drawing doodles in the dirt with her finger. Gabby sighed. "Bella's going to throw her cup on the floor."

"My mother had six children. I'm sure she's seen it all before." He slid an arm around her shoulders, the fit of her against his side altogether comfortable.

His instinct to propose a business marriage with steamy chemistry had been spot-on. And given that she didn't pull away, he was making progress.

One step at a time—the next being persuading her to move into a cabin—he would win her over to becoming his wife.

Sitting at the dinner table, Gabby felt like a lead player in *Cinderella Wore Cowgirl Boots*. But she'd survived.

For most of the meal, she stayed quiet, picked at her food and made sure her daughter didn't create a compost heap under her booster chair. Thank goodness for that makeover, though, since the gorgeous Taylor siblings collectively were an intimidating force.

True to his word, Ryan had arranged for a change of clothes, and thankfully, his sisters had done so in a way that didn't overwhelm her. By the time she returned to Ryan's home from the barn, a selection of potential outfits had been delivered. Six dresses to choose from, all casual and the type that could still be worn with her boots.

Luckily, Gabby had packed an extra outfit for Bella since toddler messes were a given on any day, but all the more for one spent playing on a ranch. And objectively speaking, of course, her daughter looked adorable in her pink overalls and fresh French braid while Ryan kept watch over her from one side and Gabby from the other.

For herself, Gabby had chosen a paisley wraparound dress that flowed down to her boots. She'd swept her hair to one side with a clip holding it to trail over one shoulder. Appearances shouldn't matter, but she couldn't stop the nerves over this first impression. She was connected to these people around the dinner table for the rest of her life through Bella— and Ryan. For both of them, she wanted the waters to be peaceful.

Or at the very least, cordial.

There wasn't anything she could do about Ryan's father's disapproval, but she wouldn't mind having as many allies as possible in the rest of his family. At least Thaddeus had been a no-show for supper. And his absence didn't seem to upset anyone in the least. That made her sad for Ryan. She understood too well the disappointment of a father's rejection.

Chatter flew at her from all angles as she righted Bella's sippy cup, trying to keep up with the conversation. Gabby had made a point of sitting by Allison, since she knew her. Ryan's brothers, Daniel and Seth, sat across from her. His sister Eloise sat next to her fiancé, Dante Sanchez, their phone set to nursery monitor mode so they could watch over their new baby sleeping upstairs. Their mother sat at one end of the table, and his sister Charlotte at the other, with her fiancé, Billy Abernathy, to her right. Gabby made a mental memo to add Billy to her notebook as brother to Robin, the woman she'd met at the bookstore.

Thankfully, the dinner hadn't been over-the-top formal. They'd eaten at a table in an enclosed sunroom, with the night stars shining in the background. The table was set with glazed pottery that looked hand thrown, the sort of dinnerware meant to be informal. But even as they drank from Mason jars, the place settings clearly cost a fortune.

Bella clanked her cup against her plate. "Gamma got nuggets. Pony nuggets."

The name Gamma was bittersweet since Gabby's mom had once dreamed of being a grandmother. But Gabby also knew her mother would want this pampering for Bella.

"Yes, she did," Gabby said softly, leaning to ease the cup from her daughter's vise grip.

On short notice, Imogen had arranged a kid-friendly, fun meal for Bella with nuggets shaped like ponies and cheese chunks cut out like little horseshoes.

Imogen adjusted her pearl necklace. "I'm glad you like them, little one. I just wish that Billy's three children could have joined us tonight, as well. Maybe next time."

As smoothly as the dinner had been served, the dishes were cleared away. By a regular housekeeper? Or caterer? Gabby didn't get a chance to ask before a dessert plate appeared in front of her—gooseberry pie with vanilla ice cream melting over the warmth.

A lull settled over the conversation—no doubt because of the mouthwatering dessert. Gabby searched for something to say, some value to add to the conversation.

Her attention landed on Dante Sanchez, who hadn't said much during the dinner. Perhaps he couldn't get a word in edgewise, either. "Dante, Ryan and I picked up carryout from your sister's restaurant last week. The Library's food is amazing."

Dante looked up from his pie with a proud smile. "Camilla is definitely a culinary genius. I'm glad that the rest of Bronco gets to enjoy her talent."

Gabby set aside her spoon. "I thought I had figured out the bulk of the family connections around Bronco, and then I find it's time to take more notes."

Soft chuckles and nods rippled from around the table.

Billy Abernathy dabbed the corner of his mouth with his napkin. "There's definitely a lot of shared history for a few key families in this region—mostly between those of us in Bronco and folks in Rust Creek Falls."

Charlotte tossed a leftover dinner roll at Billy. "There's no need to bore her with all the history of our little corner of the world."

Gabby laughed at the exchange, but rushed to reassure him, "This is Bella's heritage now, too, which makes me very interested. Please share."

"Well, since you asked so nicely, Gabby..." He leveled a gloating grin toward Charlotte. "A big part of what ties us together is the mystery about Winona's baby."

Gabby held up a hand. "Wait, that's the quirky older lady who dates Stanley Sanchez and used to write the syndicated advice column?"

Billy applauded softly. "You're a quick study. She's in her nineties now so this story goes way back. Charlotte, why don't you take it from here? I've got a roll to eat."

He held up the dinner roll that his fiancée had pitched at him earlier.

Charlotte nudged aside her dessert plate, in full storyteller mode. "When Winona Cobbs and Josiah Abernathy were teenagers in Rust Creek Falls—" she paused, nodding toward Billy to acknowledge the Abernathy family connection "—they had a secret affair. Winona got pregnant and her family institutionalized her until the baby was born. Poor Winona thought that her baby girl was stillborn. But it turns out that wasn't true. The baby was placed for adoption elsewhere."

Gabby's heart hurt in sympathy for the woman, alone and pregnant. "How truly awful."

She understood that pain well, however, even if she lived in a time when society was more accepting. But to be shuttled off to an institution? To have her baby essentially stolen from her? Gabby's hand slid to her child's back, needing to keep her close.

Charlotte smiled reassuringly. "Thankfully, that's not the end of the story. Billy's cousin Gabe Abernathy and his now wife, Melanie, somehow figured out the baby was alive—that part's a long story for another day. Basically, Josiah, still alive, had dementia and couldn't tell them where their daughter, Beatrix, was, but he indicated the child was still out there. So the two of them worked to unravel the mystery."

All thoughts of keeping notebooks on the tangled connections gave way to an emotional connection to the people of this town. "You've got me hooked. Did they find the baby?"

"They sure did," Charlotte said, crossing her arms in triumph. "Turns out Beatrix had been adopted and renamed Dorothea—Daisy. She's Evan Cruise's grandmother. Now, Winona lives in Bronco with her daughter Daisy, her secret baby."

At the words *secret baby*, Eloise kicked her sister not too subtly, which then launched a wave of awkwardness to everyone else at the table.

Might as well address the pink little elephant in the room. "Well, it's nice to know I'm not the only one with a secret-baby past."

After three heartbeats of silence, Gabby worried that she may have misjudged the sense of humor of the Taylor crowd. Then Allison pressed her hand to her mouth, a low laugh bubbling, and the rest quickly followed suit. One of the brothers—Gabby was still trying to keep them straight—even teased Ryan about being a fool to let her go.

A sigh of relief shuddered through her. She felt… accepted. And until that moment she hadn't fully grasped how important that was. Yes, the primary focus here tonight was Bella's happiness, but that would be so much easier to envision with the support of Ryan's family.

"Hello, family." Thaddeus's distinctive voice from the far end of the room slung an icy wet blanket over the levity.

Laughter faded along with smiles. Some stared at their plates, others focused on eating. Ryan glared.

His father strode into the sunroom, a trench coat slung over his arm. "Sorry to be late for this special dinner. I had an important meeting." He angled to kiss Imogen on the cheek without actually making contact. "But I'm glad to have made it in time for our cook's famous gooseberry pie."

Allison looked like she'd eaten a lemon. "Dad, you didn't need to rush away on our account."

"Careful, daughter dear," he said as he patted her on the head, "or I'm going to feel unwanted."

Allison's eyes went wide with anger as she brushed her hand over her hair, muttering, "We can't have that."

Thaddeus stopped next beside Gabby, his grin so effortless it was chilling. "Hello, Gabrielle. Thank you for joining us for dinner. Now, how about you properly introduce me to this cute little girl." He reached behind the toddler's ear, pulled out a quarter and offered her the money.

Cringing away, Bella ducked downward into her booster chair. Gabby wanted to applaud her daughter over not being for sale.

Instead, Gabby did her best to pull a smile. "This is Bella. Bella, can you say hello to, uh, to Ryan's father?"

She couldn't yet bring herself to label him Grandpa.

"Hello." The word drifted up, mumbled and muffled in the fabric.

Thaddeus patted her on the head as he'd done Allison. "We have time to visit another day." He pulled up an extra chair to sit beside his wife. "Now, let's enjoy this amazing pie. I'll take an extra scoop of ice cream."

Gabby rubbed her daughter's arm in comfort. Confusion and more than a little unease crept over her. Thaddeus's words had been benign. However, as much as she wanted to hope he'd changed his tune and decided to accept the inevitable, she couldn't ignore the fact that only a short while ago, this same man wanted to buy her off and send her away. He'd planned to cut off his own flesh and blood. That would take a lot more than a polite greeting to forgive.

At the third stop sign on his way to drive Gabby back to her apartment, Ryan couldn't wait any longer. He leaned across to kiss her, linger, just long enough to taste gooseberries and ice cream. He wanted more of her. All. But this wasn't the right time.

He angled back behind the wheel into the heated seat's embrace and accelerated into the night.

Her eyes went wide, illuminated by the orange glow from the dash. "What was that for?"

Did he need a reason? For now, it appeared he did. But he looked forward to the day they were comfortable enough around each other again for a kiss to be a natural greeting or temporary goodbye. "Because you turn me inside out."

Laughing self-consciously, she toyed with the shoulder harness of her seat belt. "You're just saying that because of the Cinderella makeover in your sister's lovely dress."

"Trust me." He leveled a glance her way before returning his attention to the road, careful to keep watch for a glimpse of deer on the side of the road ready to leap. The road was narrow. The drop-off steep. Not a forgiving landscape. "I was thinking about it long before that, when you were still in those faded jeans."

"Well, thank you, then. I accept the compliment." She tipped her head in acknowledgment. "Thank goodness I packed extra clothes for Bella."

Ryan glanced at the rearview mirror and found his daughter asleep in the car seat, head lolling forward much like their last outing together as a family. *Family.* His mouth dried right up. "I'm always surprised that she can sleep sitting up with her head like that."

"She's that tired. So am I, actually." She stifled a yawn. "The day was longer than I expected."

It was, but he still had to fight to push back the vision of crawling into bed with Gabby at the end of a long day, their child asleep in the next room. "Thank you for being flexible about dinner. That meant so much to my siblings and my mom. You and Bella charmed everyone. Well done."

She chewed her bottom lip nervously. "Your father was very polite."

"Uh, yeah." He hoped she wasn't snowed by his dad's act. Because there was no way he'd turned his attitude around that fast. Thaddeus was up to something. "I'm surprised he showed up."

"You're missing my point." She pivoted toward him in her seat, her knee hitching up. "Your father wants to pay for me to leave town, with my child— his own flesh and blood—and he appeared gracious.

How do I know if everyone else really welcomes us or if they're putting on a show like your dad?"

While he was relieved that she saw through his father's act, Ryan hadn't anticipated the lack of trust for the rest of his family. He searched for the right words to put her mind at ease.

"Good question. The answer?" He settled for the simple truth and hoped she would believe him. "Because they're not my father. When they welcome you, they mean it."

"As long as they don't hurt Bella, I can handle anything else." There was no denying the ferocity in her voice.

"With time you'll see that and be able to trust them, too." He understood her caution, but he needed her to give him time, too, in order to lower her defenses. "Have you given more thought to moving into one of the cabins?"

He thought he'd seen some thawing on the subject when he'd shown her the options during their tour of the ranch. Bella was clearly a fan of country living.

"It would certainly be more convenient," Gabby said, her tone cautious, "but still. That's such a big move and what if it doesn't work out? Leaving will make things so much more complicated for us."

Or make things far less complicated when they could recapture what they'd shared in Nashville and move forward with bringing up their daughter— under the same roof. "You're still thinking about it, though, right? The extra space, the yard, the help, the pony…"

"I'm thinking." She clapped a hand over her heart, right over the V in the wraparound dress that gaped just a hint. "I'll let you know if that status changes."

He drew his gaze upward, then back to the road just in time—he almost missed the turn into her complex. "You know I'm going to do my best to change your mind."

"How so?"

Out of the corner of his eye, he saw her long legs cross at the ankles as she stuck her booted feet under the heater's blast.

He remembered those legs well—with nothing covering them. "Is that an invitation?"

She snorted on a laugh as he threw the SUV into Park, engine idling. "Not today, cowboy."

"That gives me hope for tomorrow," he retorted, enjoying the ease of their banter, not ready for the day to end. He scanned the lot for sports car guy to make sure he hadn't parked too close, a fierce protectiveness pumping through him. But the dude's spot was empty. "Actually, there's a rodeo coming to the next county over in a week. It's small. Nothing in comparison to the Bronco Summer Family Rodeo in July, but it's still well attended by locals. I thought you and Bella might enjoy it. Maybe you'll make some new business contacts. There's even a division with a canine agility competition."

"That sounds wonderful. Let's talk tomorrow after I check my calendar." The toes of her boots flexed back and forth. "Maybe I should look into agility training for Elsie. I have to admit, it's not always easy wearing her out in the apartment during the colder days."

He gave her a pointed look.

She rolled her eyes. "Yes, I know. Another reason a cabin on your property would be helpful."

Her laugh twined with his in the enclosed space.

He skimmed a loose strand of her hair behind her ear, wondering what she would say if he kissed her again, if he followed up that kiss with a request to go inside with her.

As he started to lean toward her, he paused, giving her the chance to say no. The charged moment stretched out between them. Her breathing slowed. His heartbeat picked up speed. Then, just when his gaze dipped to her mouth, Gabby's hand fell to rest on his chest, twisting in his shirt and pulling him toward her.

Chapter Eleven

Gabby didn't know why she'd kissed Ryan.

Well, she knew *why*—he was hot.

But kissing him wasn't wise.

Although right now, in the front seat of his SUV, parked in the lot of her building, indulging in a lip-lock was safe. No risk of going too far, or concerns that she would have to answer his family's questions about their future. Safe *and* chaperoned. Their daughter was asleep in the back. They were in a public location.

Gabby's lips parted. She could steal this moment for herself. Her hands splayed against the hard wall of his chest, his muscles playing beneath her fingertips. He tasted of ice cream and memories. She was tempted. So much so, she could swear she saw stars behind her eyelids.

Except they weren't stars. The glare was from…
Headlights.

She jolted away, her fingers flying to her mouth even though the luxury sedan pulled into a spot farther down the row. "Oh my."

"Ditto," Ryan said wryly, easing back into his seat, draping his wrist over the steering wheel. "You still pack quite a punch."

"I assume that's a compliment." She drew in one shaky breath after the other to steady her heart.

"Trust me, it is."

The heater was suddenly too warm on her inflamed skin. "I guess those car lights are our sign to call it a day. Even with the surprise dinner, it was still wonderful. I enjoyed your mom and your siblings."

Was that babbling coming from her mouth?

"They were impressed with you and Bella, too. I could tell." His gaze held hers, the parking lot lamps and approaching vehicles casting shadows along the angular lines of his face.

And even though she'd said it was time to go, she didn't move. Neither did he. Bella was asleep and the evening was quiet. The world felt far away, easy enough to kick deeper concerns down the road for another day.

Right now, she just wanted to sit with him, to know more about this enigmatic man. "You seem close to your siblings."

"Some more than others. But I love them all." His smile was genuine—entrancing.

Maybe if she could learn more about him, she could figure out why she found him so difficult to resist and come up with a plan for managing their shared-custody life. "What's your favorite childhood memory? I told you about puzzles with my mom."

His smile widened. "It all goes back to those campfires and sleeping under the stars."

"As a kid?" she asked. "You mentioned that before, but I didn't realize you were that young."

He clapped a hand over his heart. "It was a rite of passage in our family."

An image of the whole family camping seemed incongruous. "I can't envision your dad—or your mom, for that matter—sleeping in a tent."

His grin went to half wattage. "We went with the foreman, or a relative, like our uncle. There were always opportunities to ride the range."

She thought of the rugged Montana landscape that stretched for miles and miles away from civilization. How easy it would be to get lost out in the wilds. "Wasn't it dangerous for a child?"

"I didn't go on long-distance cattle drives until later, but keep in mind, kids out here start rodeo young." He glanced up at the rearview mirror. "I look forward to getting Bella's first saddle—"

His words were cut short by the roar of an engine. More than just the gentle sweep of headlights. The beams, the rumble, came on quickly, aggressively. Startled, Gabby looked over her shoulder just as the growl of the high-powered engine grew louder.

Sports car guy.

The low-slung vehicle sped past, then stopped short, brakes squealing before whipping into the designated spot—inches from her minivan. Sports car guy, however, had plenty of room to exit on his driver's side.

Ryan cursed under his breath, turned off the SUV and threw open the door. "What a jerk."

Gabby lunged across to rest a hand on his elbow. "Forget about him. No need to make a scene."

"I'm just going to talk to him." Ryan swept his Stetson off the dash and dropped it on his head.

Panicked, she shot a quick look to check on her daughter and Bella was still somehow asleep in spite of the noise. Of course, on any other day if Gabby so much as opened a soda can, her daughter would have jolted awake. Thank goodness, right now Bella was out for the count.

Gabby leaped from the passenger side, sticking near her daughter but needing to know what happened, to defuse the situation if necessary.

Ryan strode with purpose toward the sleek red vehicle, not in a threatening manner but definitely authoritative. "Good evening. Mind if we have a word for a minute?"

"Sorry, man." The young executive juggled his

briefcase to the other hand and hip bumped his door closed. "I'm in a rush."

"Then I'll make this quick." Ryan hooked his thumbs in his jeans pockets. "That's my girlfriend's minivan and you've been parking so close to her, she's unable to get out of her vehicle."

Girlfriend?

The slick businessman thumbed the key fob. "Like I told her. I'm in my spot. So this is not my problem."

"Come on," Ryan said, his voice low and calm in the night, "that's not a very gentlemanly way to behave."

"So sue me." Sports car dude pivoted away and jogged up the walkway.

Ryan's jaw jutted. The restraint all but radiated from his body, like a lion eager to pounce. Then a sigh shuddered through him, his fists unclenching.

He strode back to her, slower. "Sorry for causing a scene there."

"Actually, I thought you showed great self-control." Even though he hadn't been successful in persuading the guy to be more accommodating in parking, a part of her was thankful to have Ryan's help.

So why was she resisting the cabin offer so hard? For so many reasons, it would be better for Bella, even Elsie. So what was the problem?

She didn't doubt her independence. She could— and had—taken care of her daughter on her own. So her real reasons?

Pride.

Fear.

And the kiss they'd just shared.

Obviously, keeping her distance wasn't working. She had to come up with real solutions for how to deal with Ryan's daily presence in her life. To do so, she needed to quit hiding and face things head-on.

As much as she hated to admit it, Ryan was right about the cabin. Bella would need—and deserved—every opportunity to get to know her new family members during this transition. Staying at the ranch for the remainder of her lease would also give her time to search for more family- and pet-friendly ac-commodations.

Sighing, she nodded toward her sandwiched mini-van. "Ryan, I'm ready to revisit the subject of mov-ing into one of the cabins."

When Gabby had told Ryan she would like to move into a cabin on his property after all, she hadn't ex-pected the change to happen so quickly—in less than forty-eight hours.

Now, she began sorting through boxes in the mid-dle of her brand-new, fully furnished abode—a two-bedroom, two-bath, log-style home with an office nook off the kitchen. Maybe she shouldn't have been surprised at how quickly Ryan arranged for the move into the cabin, given how eager he'd been to relo-cate her. But once she gave him the go-ahead, packers were on her doorstep the next morning. They'd boxed up the essentials right away, with the plan to put the rest in storage.

Moving was definitely easier with an unlimited budget and a baby daddy who kept his toddler offspring entertained on moving day.

She cut into a packing box marked Dishes and lifted out a plate to unwrap from the packing paper. She set it on the pine table and started on another.

Decorated with a rustic vibe, the cabin was exactly the sort of place she'd envisioned finding for herself, Bella and Elsie when she'd begun making her plans to move to Montana. A fat leather sectional sofa filled the living room; a split log table with benches delineated the eating area. The fence around the back of the cabin looked suspiciously new, but Elsie was loving sprinting around and sniffing.

Ryan had gone above and beyond with personal touches, as well. A toddler bed had been added to the second bedroom, with a new stuffed unicorn perched on the pillow. Pink cowgirl boots and a matching hat rested on the dresser.

But the most moving touch of all? In Gabby's room, on her brass bed, waited a stack of brand-new jigsaw puzzles. How could she not be charmed by a man who gave such thoughtful gifts—not focusing on the money but on her preferences?

She skimmed her fingers along the textured planks

of the table, pausing from the dish unwrapping for a moment to consider which puzzle she would start. The Montana mountain-scape, the Americana quilt collage or the herd of horses running through a stream. Had he chosen them himself or relegated the purchase to an assistant?

Caught in her reverie, she almost missed the sound of the front door opening. Surprised, she set aside the plate she'd begun to unwrap and turned to find...

Thaddeus Taylor? What was he doing here?

Her throat went dry with nerves. "Good afternoon. If you're looking for Ryan, he's with Bella at the stables. I think he was going to take her on a short ride."

He stepped deeper into the living room, sweeping his Stetson from his head. "You've settled right in."

Thaddeus was dressed more casually today than the other times she'd seen him. However, even in jeans and flannel, he was no less intimidating.

Of course, that could have something to do with the fact that he'd offered to pay her off if she and Bella left town. Or maybe it had more to do with him entering her home without so much as a knock. She bristled before taking a deep breath to respond more calmly. "Ryan has been very helpful with the move."

"You seem uneasy," he said, his smile not in the least comforting. "I imagine my son told you of my... concerns."

Her breath caught in her throat. "That's for you and Ryan to discuss."

"What a diplomatic response," he said with be-grudging approval. "Protecting my family legacy is everything to me. And while you seem like a lovely young lady, you and my son come from very different worlds."

"I'm aware." What was he trying to accomplish?

"Now that you have made yourself comfortable in this rent-free home—" he paused, looking around the cabin at the stacks of boxes "—I see you're playing the long game in trapping my son."

Trapping? How dare he speak to her this way! "Mr. Taylor, that's enough. I'm not comfortable with this conversation. Any relationship—or lack thereof—between myself and Ryan is our business. Not yours."

He sat on the arm of the sofa, his eyes laser focused on her. "In case my son didn't tell you about the conversation he and I had, I'll cut to the chase. How much will it cost me for you and your child to leave Bronco, Montana, for good?"

She stiffened her spine, hating how his sitting there, dominating the space, made her feel like a kid in the principal's office. But she wasn't going to fall for his power play. "How about I cut to the chase, as well? I'm not for sale. And neither is my child."

"Understood." He nodded, then stood, closing the space between them, towering over her. "But you need to understand me as well, my dear. When I talk about protecting the Taylor legacy from scandal, from the disgrace of illegitimacy, know that I will do anything, anything at all, to protect my son. Surely, as a parent you can understand that."

She refused to back away. "*You* need to understand *me*. You are the only one here disgracing himself. Now please leave."

The standoff lasted for at least four heartbeats, maybe not that long since her heart was pounding fast with adrenaline-fueled anger.

Finally—thank goodness, finally—he moved, putting distance between them. He paused at the door to deliver his final shot. "Let me know if you change your mind. The offer and my checkbook are open."

The door clicked softly after him. Her knees folded and she sank onto the wooden bench, her hands shaking in the aftermath. She'd traded sports car guy for a far more menacing presence.

She'd been told Thaddeus was unkind, devious even. But she'd seen a cruelty in his eyes that made her heart hurt thinking of Ryan growing up around such toxicity. No wonder he struggled with relationships. Was that something he could recover from or had his father's behavior hardwired Ryan to avoid attachments?

Nerves knocked around in her stomach. She reminded herself of the puzzles, of how Ryan had worked so hard to connect with Bella. He'd said before that he had trust issues.

Now, as she sat here scared to her toes at the prospect of getting hurt, she realized she had more than a few trust issues of her own.

Today was a dream that Ryan hadn't even known he wanted.

The sun was shining. He'd saddled up Buzz for a ride. And his child was strutting confidently beside him, at home in the stable. She was a dusty mess from playing in the dirt and her braid had come halfway undone.

She was a bona fide country girl. "One horse. Two horse," she chanted. "Three horse. Four horse…"

"Are you ready to go for a ride with me on Buzz?" The palomino was his gentlest from the stable. He'd arranged a helmet for Bella as well, a symbol of how he would do anything to keep her safe.

She nodded fast. "Yes, pwease."

"If you get scared, just say so and we'll stop." Was he asking too much of her? He didn't know much about kids this age. Gabby had told him it would be fine, but to watch for trepidation.

"Not scared," Bella said, fiddling with the strap on her helmet. "Wanna ride Buzz."

"Alrighty, then. Here we go." He waved for a stable hand to assist. Ryan swung up into the saddle, then extended his arms for Bella to be passed up. He nodded his thanks, then turned his attention to watching Bella.

Sitting astride Buzz with Bella in front of him, he

bracketed his child with his strong arms. She leaned back against his chest, so tiny, yet so fearless.

He loved this kid with every fiber of his being.

He didn't want to think in terms of winning and losing. But he couldn't deny the sense of victory over having Gabby and Bella move onto the ranch.

Clicking the horse into motion, he kept the pace slow. They wouldn't go far, just over to the cabin. The gentle roll of the horse and clop, clop of hooves along the beaten path drew a giggle from Bella. He dipped his head to see her face and found her toying with a piece of jewelry around her neck. It looked like…a pearl necklace?

At first he wondered if she wore something of his mother's but then realized this was a more delicate strand than his mother favored. "Where did you get the necklace, Bella?"

"Found it. Me pwetty," she said proudly.

It must be Gabby's. He would pass it over when they saw her.

His cell phone rang in his pocket. He wanted to ignore it, but the ringtone was one he reserved for his siblings. An arm locked around Bella, he accepted the call, thankful he'd thought to wear an earbud. "Hello?"

"Hey there, little brother," Daniel's voice echoed through.

He ignored the "little" comment. "Everything okay? No offense, but I'm busy."

He kept an eye on Bella as she gently stroked Buzz's silky mane.

"I was just checking to make sure you're still alive," Daniel said, poking fun at him. "We haven't seen you around the office much lately."

"In case you hadn't noticed, life threw me a curveball." To be honest, he was surprised at how easy it had been to put work out of his mind lately—unusual for him. He nudged Buzz with his knee to bypass a pothole in the path.

"I can tell, since nothing ever distracts you from work. Everything's covered, though. No worries," Daniel assured him. "Did Gabby get settled into the cabin?"

"The movers brought over everything they need—clothes, toys and such." And if he had his way, she would be moving again soon—into his house. "They'll move the furniture to storage to sort through later if she wants to swap out some of the cabin decor for her own."

"Sounds like you've got it covered. Let me know if she needs help."

"While I have you on the phone," Ryan said, coming to a decision, "I'm going to take some more personal time. I need to get things started on the right foot with Gabby and Bella." He wanted more days like this with his daughter. Even though Gabby was still working, he wanted to be available for Bella... and whenever Gabby was free. This time was a golden opportunity to win her over, an opportunity he couldn't afford to squander.

"Hmm," Daniel mused. "Are you picking up where you two left off back in Nashville?"

Might as well make his plans known. His family needed to understand how serious he was about committing to Bella and Gabby. "If I have my way, yes. She's still not ready to make that leap."

"I imagine she's worried for her kid if things don't work out between the two of you. Mom and Dad aren't exactly a testament to a Taylor Happily-Ever-After," Daniel said dryly. "Good luck."

The call disconnected, and as if conjured from the negative vibes, Thaddeus drove toward them on the dirt path, his SUV kicking up dust behind him. Had his father been visiting Gabby? If so, why? Whatever his reason, it couldn't be good.

He eyed her cabin in the distance, the one closest to his house—not a coincidence. Smoke puffed from the chimney. Elsie trotted around the yard like a queen, her tail sweeping side to side in happy wags.

He had to grin at Gabby's minivan parked there with tons of free space on either side. For now, he would focus on the victory and worry about the rest later.

Buzz clopped the last few strides to the log cabin's newly installed fence. Gabby stood silhouetted in the doorway, jeans showcasing her shapely legs, a long-sleeved T-shirt hugging her gentle curves.

He cued the horse to stop as Gabby walked up alongside them, shading her eyes. "Look at the two of you."

She reached out her arms for Ryan to pass Bella down.

"Mommy, Mommy, Mommy, I rided." Excitement rang from every syllable.

"I saw." Gabby hugged Bella close. Protectively? "Did you tell Dada thank you?"

Bella grinned, looking too cute in her pink helmet. "Tank you."

"You're welcome," he said, dismounting and looping Buzz's reins around the fence post. "Anytime."

"Be careful or she'll be asking you every day." She set Bella on her feet and unclipped the helmet.

"That's fine with me." This was as good a time as any to let her know he would be around more. "I've taken a couple of weeks' personal time to help you two settle in."

Her gaze swung to his, surprised and newly assessing.

"You didn't have to do that—but I'm glad you did," she said, the wind lifting her light brown hair. "For Bella's sake, of course."

"Of course," he answered, even as he knew it was so much more than that for both of them now. But it served no purpose to push the point. "I saw my dad leaving the cabin. What did he want?"

Her lengthy pause, her fast blinking eyes, all relayed stress. "He just stopped by to say hello."

What had his father done? From the way she looked all around him rather than at him, Ryan could tell she wasn't interested in sharing.

He didn't want to wreck the day for her. He would just ask his father later. "Hey, before I forget, Bella has a necklace on. I believe it's yours. I figured she must have picked it up in all the moving mayhem."

Frowning, Gabby knelt to her daughter and lifted the pearl necklace. Looking at the strand resting against her fingers, she shook her head. She unclasped it from Bella's neck. "That's not mine. Bella, where did you find this?"

Bella looked at her solemnly, then pointed to the barn.

"Well, sweetie, it doesn't belong to us. I'll let you play with some of my jewelry, though. We can make a little box for you." Gabby passed the pearl strand to Ryan.

He tucked it into his pocket. "Maybe it belongs to my mom or one of my sisters, even? Plenty of people come through here. I'll ask around later." Then a thought struck him of his mother's jewelry and how much she glowed when another gift box arrived. The puzzles suddenly seemed like a pathetic offering. "Did you like the necklace?"

"It's a pretty piece, but not something I need," she rushed to assure him. "You've already given me a cabin—and the most thoughtful puzzles. Thank you." She arched up on her toes to kiss his cheek.

So easy. So natural, like they'd been together for years. Her pure spirit was a rarity, something he didn't deserve but couldn't imagine letting go.

She said she wanted more than a convenient relationship. His experience in that department was lacking, and if he didn't figure out how to fake it soon, he could lose her for good. For her and for Bella, he needed to figure out how to pretend to be the family guy Gabby wanted and pray she didn't see through his act.

Chapter Twelve

A couple of weeks ago, Gabby never could have imagined going on a family outing with Ryan and Bella with the whole town of Bronco knowing their secret. But now that they'd made an announcement on social media, what better place to finish spreading the word than at a rodeo—even one in the next county over.

Ryan kept Bella on his shoulders, her pink boots a sweet contrast against his flannel shirt as they made their way from their VIP box seats toward the concession stand.

The stadium was a cacophony of sounds. The loudspeaker blasting commentary on the events, with a low undercurrent of country tunes. Cheers and gasps rippling from the crowd. Chuffing and pawing echoing from horses, bulls and calves. The steady thud of Ryan's boots reminding her of his presence beside her.

And so many eyes on them, gossip all but humming over the attendees in a cloud of interest.

Pausing on a step to let others pass, Gabby looked up at Ryan, his blue eyes mesmerizing in their excitement. "I'm so glad you suggested this. If this is a small rodeo, I can only imagine how big the Bronco one will be this summer." Would they attend that one together, as well? "I go to rodeos for business quite often, but getting to come for pure pleasure is different—better. And I've most definitely never had seats like yours."

"A family perk," he said with a wink. "You and Bella will have the best seats in the house for the rest of your lives."

"Bella is a Taylor," she reminded him—and herself. "I am not."

His gaze held hers, the connection crackling between them. "You know I'm willing to change that whenever you're ready. Just say the word."

"Shh." She arched up on her toes, her finger to her lips. "Someone might hear you."

He grinned with no sign of repentance. "I'm not making a secret of what I want for our future. Is that so wrong of me?"

The sparkle inside her faded as the flirting turned entirely too serious. "A loveless marriage is a disaster in the making," she reminded him, then forced a smile. "But thank you for the offer."

Living in the cabin was plenty close enough. Although she had to admit, it had been helpful having him nearby. He'd even driven Bella to daycare when Gabby had had an early morning meeting.

Ryan was a good neighbor—a good father.

She sighed, and his aftershave teased her nose, overriding the rodeo scents blended into an earthy perfume of leather and smoke from the barbecue puffing a mouthwatering aroma from a distance.

"Hey," she said, working to pull her focus off tempting thoughts, "did you ever find out who the pearl necklace belonged to?"

He shook his head. "I asked around the ranch and checked to make sure it wasn't Mom's or my sisters'. But no luck. So I took it to a jeweler in town to see if it's the real deal before going any further."

"That's too bad," she said, just as another tempting whiff of his aftershave drifted through her senses.

So much for small talk.

The bottleneck eased and they were able to step forward again, descending the concrete steps. Hand after hand clapped Ryan on the shoulder, before each passing person waved at her with undisguised interest. Some faces she knew, others looked familiar but she couldn't place the name. Still, there was time to get to know them. Even if she only stayed at the cabin for the rest of the year, Bronco was her hometown now.

Bella drummed her boot heels against Ryan's chest. "Wanna see puppies. Pwease."

They'd tried to explain about the dog agility event, but Bella somehow thought they were going back to the Tenacity shelter to see puppies. "Soon, sweetie," Gabby said. "We are going to watch grown-up dogs play and jump once we get our lunch."

The buzz of chatter increased as the barbecue scent grew stronger. Ryan guided her toward the line. He'd told her earlier he could have had food delivered to their seats, but concessions and the surrounding picnic tables were the best place to socialize. She was committed to ending the rumors about their relationship and showing the town that they were a family, albeit a nontraditional one. Amicable co-parenting was something to be proud of, as far as she was concerned.

Gabby felt a hand on her elbow and looked back to find a lovely woman standing behind her. "Pardon me, I just have to say that your little girl is adorable."

Ryan cupped Bella's boots and sent an affectionate look at Gabby. "She's a little firecracker, just like her mother."

If Ryan was trying to kick the gossip into overdrive, he was sure doing all the right things.

Gabby extended her hand. "I don't think we've met. I'm Gabby Hammond. I just recently moved to

Bronco. This is my daughter, Bella, and her father, Ryan."

"I'm Tori Hawkins." Tori folded her hand in a welcoming grip, then glanced at Ryan. "One of Suzie and Arthur's five kids."

Ah, right. Tori competed in rodeos like her parents. Gabby had heard about the Hawkins family— *all* rodeo stars.

Ryan thumped himself on the forehead. "Right, Tori, I heard you were in town again after your latest tour. Welcome back." He shot a glance at Gabby. "Tori's grandma Hattie was quite a trailblazer on the rodeo circuit back in the day."

"Your grandmother sounds like a *true* firecracker and great role model for the rest of her family." Gabby crinkled her nose. "And here I was thinking you were a newbie in town like me. I'm considering starting a notebook to keep up with everyone."

Tori laughed, elbowing her gently. "I may want to borrow it. Even I have trouble keeping up. Nice to meet you." She waved to the concessions counter. "Don't let me keep you from getting your lunch."

Gabby turned back to the counter as Ryan passed Bella to her. After placing their order, he carried their tray piled with fried pickles, a funnel cake, barbecue turkey leg and chicken wings. Bella had chosen the chicken nugget on a stick with fries—no surprise. They settled at a picnic table tucked in a corner near a sheepshearing contest.

They ate together in companionable silence while Bella babbled and pointed.

Dropping a chicken wing, Gabby licked her fingers and sighed. "This is so good."

His eyes lingered on her mouth and his throat moved in a slow swallow. "Uh, yes, but not quite as good as the ones at Doug's. It's a hole-in-the-wall bar where everyone knows your name. There is also a legend of a haunted barstool there that causes tragedy to anyone who sits on it." He pinched off a bite from the funnel cake. "When I take you there on a date, I'll make sure we avoid the cursed seat."

A date? That was different from a family outing. But she couldn't bring herself to correct him. Maybe it was the way his heated gaze made her stomach flip.

Ryan set down his half-eaten turkey leg. "When we came in, as I looked at the canine agility course, it made me think of Elsie. She doesn't have to be competing to enjoy it. I could add a little dog park of sorts on the ranch, with a pole to jump over, posts to weave through like a barrel racer."

What a thoughtful idea for her dog. In spite of all her boundary making and resolve not to let him charm her, she found herself touched by his efforts.

She broke off a bite of the shared funnel cake. "I wouldn't want you to go to all that trouble for me. Just because I'm at the cabin now during this transition doesn't mean we're staying there forever."

He grunted noncommittally, then continued as if

she hadn't spoken, "I think I could help work with her. I have horse training skills and basic dog training knowledge, so I've been reading up on nuances. We can consult with a trainer. Maybe Bella might like to learn to cue Elsie, as well."

"What if Elsie stinks at it?" The picture he painted sounded delightful, though.

"Then we'll still have fun. And so will she." He reached across the table to thumb the corner of her mouth. "Powdered sugar, from the funnel cake."

Could life really be this good? This uncomplicated? Strange to think that before she'd been dumped by Bradford, she'd dreamed of this, had been able to ignore her father's abandonment and believe in forever. Now? It didn't feel that simple to believe this neutral ground they'd found would last.

What if what his father and Nora had said was true? That Ryan's lifestyle and money were too high profile for someone like her, who preferred a simpler life? Did he need more excitement, competition, high stakes in his life? "Do you miss competing?"

A dimple kicked into one cheek and he nudged his Stetson back with a knuckle. "I still throw my hat in the ring on occasion."

"That's something I would enjoy seeing." Her skin tingled in excitement at just the thought. No doubt, he would be mesmerizing in the ring.

"That can be arranged," he said as he caught Bella's sippy cup in midair after she tossed it. "It's not too early to start Bella riding on a pony, getting used to the animals."

Bella waved her pink cowgirl hat in the air, fringe rippling on the arms of her jacket. "Yeehaw!"

Gabby surrendered to the moment, to the joy, her laughter mingling with Ryan's until handclapping from behind pulled her attention away. She turned fast to find Winona Cobbs, the lady who'd seen them in the park that day.

The fire starter of the gossip. And Winona wasn't alone. She held hands with her gentleman friend, Stanley Sanchez. The two of them looked too cute for words in their matching Western gear. If their besotted gazes were anything to judge by, romance most definitely didn't have an age limit.

Stanley pulled off his Stetson and held it to his chest as they stopped beside the picnic table. "Sorry to interrupt your meal, but my Winona wanted to say hello."

Ryan motioned for them to sit. "No need to apologize. I've been wanting an opportunity to introduce you to my daughter, Bella, and my girlfriend, Gabby."

There was that *girlfriend* word again. Not that arguing would help. "Nice to meet you, ma'am. I've heard so many delightful things about you."

Ryan stuffed his hands into his pockets. "Have you set the date for the wedding?"

Stanley gave a sheepish grin. "We haven't picked

yet. I keep asking Winona if she's having second thoughts. And she says—"

"We must wait till the time is right. Love can't be rushed." She patted his hand held in hers. "It *will* not be rushed."

What wise words. Except love wasn't a part of the equation for Gabby and Ryan. He'd never mentioned the word—and she hadn't dared think it.

Ryan needed to understand that no matter how charming and helpful he might be, pushiness would only send her running. Like Winona, Gabby would let no man dictate her timetable.

Was Gabby avoiding him?

He couldn't be certain, but it felt like she'd kept her distance since the rodeo. At least she had been true to her word about giving him unlimited access to Bella.

Although he hadn't expected access would include taking his daughter to get a haircut. Bella sat in the beautician's chair, with a black cape draped over her while hair salon owner Denise Sanchez combed through the baby-fine brown hair.

In fact, he had Bella for the whole day today. Alone. His first time watching her for this long. He'd come to pick Bella up and drive her to daycare, only to find it had been closed due to staffing illness. Gabby assured him it would be fine. She was working from home.

He'd almost left, except alarms went off in his

head. Gabby had been jittery, frazzled even. Her movements were jerky and her hands shaking. He'd pressed the point, and she'd finally confessed she had important meetings online and was worried about Bella not understanding the need to be quiet or wait to have a juice cup refilled.

Ryan had insisted on taking her for the day. He could keep her occupied—and yes, even take her for her haircut appointment that he remembered seeing on the calendar for the end of the day.

He hadn't thought this through, though. He was still a rookie at the parenting deal. But no. He'd been cocky, insisting he could handle things like a simple haircut. Yet if he hadn't drunk four cups of coffee, he would have fallen asleep right here, right now, sitting in an empty chair at the next station.

Denise pumped the chair higher for better access, the hydraulics hissing in sync with a hair dryer in the corner. "So, Ryan, I hear you saw *Tio* Stanley and Winona at the rodeo the other day. They were impressed with Gabby. Winona said she seems like a real keeper."

Wincing, Ryan snapped a photo of Bella to text to Gabby and stifled a sneeze at a cloud of hairspray wafting over from two stations down. "I find it interesting that Winona is so eager to marry others off when she's reluctant to make the walk down the aisle herself."

"Isn't that the truth?" Denise laughed as she

combed out a length of hair and snipped the very ends. "I never thought I'd see the day where you would be bringing a little one in for her haircut. How are you holding up, Dad?"

He had to confess, he was exhausted. They'd gone horseback riding, out to lunch at Bronco Burgers. She'd fallen asleep in the car and he missed the peace of her afternoon nap. Which meant she was cranky so he took her toy shopping. Yes, he knew buying her a princess doll with a horse and carriage was a bribe, but he was in a "peace at any price" mode. "We packed a lot into the day, but I'm exactly where I want to be."

And he meant it. This was his daughter and his future took on a new clarity with Bella in the picture.

Denise spun the seat a half turn to work on the other side. "What are you two doing after you leave here?"

Bella looked up so quickly, only Denise's savvy move kept her from cutting off a chunk of hair. "Pway wif ants and buckles."

Denise passed a safety lollipop to Bella to entice her to sit still. "Ants and buckles?"

A few weeks ago, he wouldn't have stood a chance at interpreting her baby talk. Now he knew that Bella meant. "Aunts and uncles. We're going to hang out with one of my brothers and one of my sisters."

Licking her sucker, Bella's face scrunched in confusion. "Do I got a brother? A sissy?"

Denise's eyebrows shot upward and he could have sworn the whole shop went quiet and still.

"No, kiddo," Ryan rushed to assure her—and everyone listening in, including the woman sweeping up hair that didn't exist just to get closer, "you're our only baby."

Denise laughed softy. "So, Dad, is the hair length right?" She turned the chair in a slow 360. "Or should I take off a little more before I start drying?"

Panic sucker punched him like a horse kick. How would he know the right length? But one thing he did know for certain. He was ready to leave. "Looks perfect, Denise. Thank you. And no need to dry it. We're late to go see the ants and buckles."

He whipped out his wallet and peeled off more than enough cash to cover the cut with a generous tip. Denise had barely taken the cape off Bella before Ryan scooped up his daughter, encouraging her to wave to everyone as he bolted out the door.

Denise's voice echoed after him. "Be sure to pull up the hood on her windbreaker so she doesn't catch a cold."

Once in the car, he turned up the heater for good measure even though it was nothing more than a windbreaker-weather day and the sun had only just started its downward move. He surrendered to turning on the video player, letting her watch her favorite unicorn videos the whole way back to the ranch.

He had the theme song memorized.

Her smile when he sang along at the top of his lungs made all the exhaustion of the day worth it.

His cell phone rang, the system cutting through Bella's video. Her bottom lip quivered.

"Don't worry," he said, fumbling for his cell, "I'll fix it." And he liked being able to do that for her.

He disabled the Bluetooth on his phone and tucked in an earbud. "Hello?"

"Son," his father's voice barked unceremoniously through the earpiece, "I know you took personal time, but I expected you to at least work remotely. What's this I hear about you *babysitting* all day?"

Ryan ground his teeth and gave himself a five count before responding. "It's not babysitting when the child is your own. I realize that may not be obvious to you." He couldn't stop himself from jabbing at his dad. Usually, he tried to ignore him, but since Bella had come into their lives, Ryan found it impossible to understand how his father could be so distant. So controlling.

Which reminded him. "Dad, what did you say to Gabby at the cabin to upset her?"

"Ask her," Thaddeus retorted, then paused. "Oh, you already have and she wouldn't tell you. How, then, will you be able to trust my answer?"

His dad's callousness blew his mind. Made him mad. And yeah, hurt. The mama bear leading her two cubs along the side of the road had better parenting instincts than his old man. "You realize that's twisted, right?"

Thaddeus sighed heavily. "I simply made sure you'd relayed my message for a large settlement if she leaves town."

Hurt and anger shifted to full-blown rage. Ryan should have known his father would pull a stunt like this. But still, how dare he? "This is the last time I'm going to tell you. Stop interfering in my life."

Or what? What could he do to stop his father? He had to come up with something, though, because this behavior could not continue.

"I'll give Gabrielle credit for one thing," Thaddeus said with begrudging admiration. "She's persistent. Look how she wore you down so quickly getting herself into free lodging. I should have done more to stop her when she got pregnant."

His blood chilled icy cold with realization. Gabby had insisted she tried to contact him, sending letters to the office while he was overseas. The answer was so obvious he should have seen it sooner. "More to stop her? You intercepted her letters to me when she found out she was pregnant."

He didn't have to ask. He knew. The only question? Would his father admit it?

"Of course I did," his father answered without hesitation or remorse. "I've never hidden who I am or what I want."

Ryan hung up before he said something he regretted. Or rather, scratch that. He wouldn't regret it. He just didn't want Bella to pick up on the anger and toxicity.

He pulled off to the side of the road to collect himself before he started driving again. If he were the only one in the car, he would barrel straight to his father and confront him face-to-face. Because his old man had cost him two years with his daughter. Two years that he could have been a meaningful part of her life. Special years he would never get back. And Ryan didn't have any idea how he'd forgive that.

But he couldn't afford to let those emotions get the better of him now. Not with Bella in the car. Safety took on a whole new meaning.

Thank goodness he was meeting up with a couple of his siblings at his house because he needed time to get his head together before Gabby would pick up Bella. He needed a plan of action for how to deal with his dad. A way to stop his father's hurtful interference before Thaddeus Taylor ruined Ryan's relationship with Gabby and Bella. His chest ached just thinking about that possibility.

First and foremost, however, Ryan needed to apologize to Gabby.

Chapter Thirteen

"Bella, would you like me to read another book?" Gabby asked in desperation, whipping a stack of hardbacks from the corner shelf.

"Noooooo," Bella wailed, sitting in the middle of her toddler bed with big fat tears running down her face. "Don't wanna go to sweep."

Dragging in three deep breaths, Gabby searched for calm. Her daughter's bedtime ritual usually took about an hour from start to finish. Bath, pj's, books, prayers, then, thankfully, sleep.

Not tonight.

They were going on ninety minutes with no sign of slumber. The last half hour had been an interminable slide from toddler restlessness to a full-blown tantrum.

When she picked up Bella from Ryan's house after the haircut, he'd warned that she'd missed her nap. Their daughter had been a whirl of frenetic, over-stimulated energy. Gabby vaguely recalled Ryan mentioning he needed to talk to her, but that it clearly wasn't the right time. Bella was jumping on the sofa while Elsie turned backflips in front of the fireplace.

Gabby had thanked Ryan and rushed out the door, exhausted from a day full of Zoom meetings. She'd foolishly crossed her fingers that Bella would be so worn out she would fall asleep quickly. No such luck.

Now, Gabby searched her depleted well of parenting tips to calm her child. Her gaze landed on the basket of stuffed animals. "What if I get you another toy?"

"Noooooo," she cried again, pitching her favorite unicorn onto the floor and drumming her legs against the mattress. "No want a toy. No want a book. No want you."

Wow. That stung. Except Gabby knew her daughter didn't mean it. But she was running out of ideas of what Bella did need. Gabby had checked her temperature. Changed her diaper. Offered her a potty break. A last glass of water. Read four books—long ones—never skipping a page to speed things along.

She'd tried everything. Bella must just be over-tired and sleep was the only solution.

Sighing, Gabby swept a gentle hand over her daughter's damp hair, kissed her forehead and backed toward the door. "All right, then, I'll turn on your night-night music. But, sweetie, you need to go to sleep."

If the crying continued, she would return to check on her and pat her back. Reassure her. Help her chill out enough to get the rest she needed.

A sniffling sounded, followed by a gulp. "Want Dada. Want Dada. Want Dada! Kiss night-night."

Gabby stopped in her tracks. Her heart melted, and she felt decidedly close to tears herself. She knelt beside Bella's bed and clasped her tiny hand. "I'll call him and see if he can come over."

Smiling, Bella wriggled under the covers, pulled the poofy bedspread up to her chin and held her arms out for a hug. "Tank you."

Gabby gathered her close, breathing in the scent of baby shampoo and sweetness. She would call Ryan to come over, although she suspected Bella would fall asleep in seconds now that the storm seemed to have passed.

Relieved to her toes, Gabby clicked on the lullaby music and stepped out of the room to get her cell phone and the nursery monitor, both charging on the kitchen counter.

The second the door clicked shut, Bella started wailing again.

Really?

Did the kid not trust her to follow through?

Gabby shook her head for being silly. Exhaustion must be messing with her mind. Bella was just being a toddler and Gabby knew what to do next. Thank goodness she didn't have to handle this on her own. It felt good to have help. Today was a hopeful example of how she and Ryan could tag-team parenting.

She unplugged her cell and the monitor, then crossed to the back door to let Elsie have a quick run around the yard. The mini-Aussie sped out in a ball of fur as if she'd had enough of the tension.

"I agree, girl," Gabby said, following to lean against a porch post. Breathing in the peaceful mountain air, she thumbed a call to Ryan.

He picked up on the first ring. "Good evening, beautiful."

His compliment caught her unaware—and warmed her weary soul. "Bella is having a meltdown."

"What's going on?" His voice shifted from low and sexy to stark and concerned. "Is she sick? I'll drive you both to the emergency room—"

"She's not sick," Gabby rushed to reassure him. "No fever, no symptoms. She's a toddler, having a temper tantrum."

"Oh, okay." His exhale echoed in her ear. "That's a relief."

"Yes, but it's still pretty awful." She thrust a hand through her tangled hair. "She wants you to come over and give her a night-night kiss." At his silence, she added, "I'm sorry to bug you and if you're busy—"

"No, it's okay. I'm just really touched," he said,

voice hoarse with emotion. "This is one of the reasons we decided for you to move closer."

And then he materialized in the moonlight, striding toward her and stealing her breath with every step closer. She clutched the phone and glanced at his log-style home in the distance. "How are you already here?"

"I started over as soon as I knew you needed me."

Thank goodness she was leaning against the porch post or she would have been wobbly at his words, his voice, his prompt caring. He opened the fence and strode closer, Elsie trotting alongside him.

He climbed the planked steps, pausing inches away from her. She disconnected the call and he tucked his phone into his pocket. The porch light cast a halo glow around them.

The tender concern on his face moved her. It was everything she'd hoped for her daughter when she dreamed of him being a part of her life. And she would let the beauty of that settle in later. When she could hear herself think.

"Thank you for coming so fast." Was that breathy voice her own? "I know I shouldn't give in to tantrums, but it's not like she asked for extra cookies. She just wants to be with you."

"Thank you for calling." He skimmed her hair behind her ear, his hand lingering for an instant to cup her jaw. "I'm glad she wants me here. I don't take that for granted."

"Glad to hear it." Her mouth went dry and she swallowed before saying, "I saved all the longest books for you."

His chuckle as he followed her inside lingered in her mind all the way to Bella's room. How easy it would be to surrender to the beauty of simple family moments like this.

Ryan was exhausted—and hopeful.

After reading Bella a final book, he'd kissed her forehead and tucked the covers under her chin, her eyes already sliding closed. He and Gabby walked to the nursery door together, his hand low on her back as they sneaked a final look at their child.

Had his parents ever enjoyed such a moment like this? Maybe early in their marriage after Daniel was born. He struggled with imagining it.

He shoved the thought away and sagged onto the sofa with Gabby, side by side, their legs pressed against each other. Her head fell to rest on his shoulder.

How right it felt to be here with her. He wondered yet again what might have happened if her letters had reached him. He knew without question that he would have proposed and even if she would have turned him down, he would have been a part of their lives from the very start of Gabby's pregnancy journey. During those two years, would he have been able to persuade her they should be together? He would never know, because his father had stolen that opportunity from both of them—from Bella, too.

He clasped Gabby's hand, resting their clasped fingers on his thigh. "I need to tell you something. My father admitted to intercepting your letters to me about being pregnant."

She nodded slowly against his shoulder. "I suspected that might be the case once I met him. It makes me sad to know he would do that, but at least now we know." She tipped her face toward him, squeezing his hand. "I'm sorry for doubting you."

He hadn't expected an apology from her. All day long he'd been eager to deliver an apology of his own. This woman was so much kinder than he deserved. "I can understand why you would think the worst of me. We barely knew each other. I'm sorry that I didn't realize sooner that it must have been my dad. I apologize for what he did to us and to Bella."

"You don't have to apologize for your dad. What he says and does is on him. I'm starting to see that with Thaddeus as a parent, trust would truly be difficult."

Her words sent a bolt of relief through him, and he realized that until this moment, he'd worried she might blame him for his father's actions. "I still feel awful for what he did. And being here on the ranch makes it all the harder to avoid him."

"At least he hasn't blocked in my minivan yet." She crinkled her nose and her eyes danced.

She was so beautiful in the dim light of the fireplace she took his breath away. Her tousled hair called to mind memories of Nashville. And not just of making love, but of strolling through Riverfront Park together, the wind whipping strands of hair across her face. Of touring the Johnny Cash museum, where she spontaneously broke out into song. Of sharing a pizza at a tavern featuring live country music. The week had been magical, memorable.

So why hadn't he called her afterward? He'd had her number. Could he have been afraid of all they'd shared? "You're giving me more grace than I deserve."

She traced her fingers along his cheek in a feather-light touch. As her gaze held his, her pupils widened with an awareness that echoed inside him. He wasn't sure who moved first, but her lips were on his. Her kiss set his blood on fire, more than any other woman's ever had. Except right now, Gabby was absolutely the only female on his mind. And he wanted her, in his arms, in his bed, in his life. And from the way her hands were running over his chest, tugging at the buttons of his chambray shirt, he had hope she felt the same way he did.

Then she swung her leg over to straddle his lap, her arms looping around his neck. She whispered against his mouth, "Take me to bed."

"Are you sure?" he asked, even though holding back was almost killing him. His heart pounded in his chest like he'd run a marathon. The feel of her curves under his hands, against him as she faced him, turned him inside out.

"Do I want you? Of course I do." She slid from his lap and stood, clasping his hand. "That's never been in doubt. So I'll say it again. Take me to bed."

All doubt wiped aside, he swept her into his arms and carried her down the hall, determined to make it a night to remember.

And to persuade her they should spend all their nights together.

Gabby woke in her bed, Ryan sleeping next to her, disoriented, not sure how much time had passed. Was it morning? Could Bella walk in on them? Panicked, she looked around the room frantically, relieved to find that moonlight streamed through the slats in the window blinds and that the nursery monitor in the corner showed her child snoozed on.

Still, Gabby feared she'd made a huge mistake.

Making love with Ryan had been even better than she remembered. Her body hummed in the aftermath of the careful attention of his touch. Of his mouth. The scent of their lovemaking still clung to the sheets in a heady perfume that stirred her senses all over again.

They'd been careful with birth control, although it panicked her more than a little to think of how "careful" hadn't worked for them last time. The timing now, though, made it even more unlikely that she would get pregnant. Although the thought of having Ryan's child again filled her with a yearning she didn't expect and couldn't embrace.

Staring at his beard-stubbled face on the pillow next to her filled her heart, so much so that it brought tears to her eyes. She snuggled closer against his side and rested her head against his chest. His strong heartbeat thudded. She trailed her fingers along his collarbone, the feel of him somehow familiar and new all at once.

She wanted the luxury of spending more nights in his bed, days in his arms. But after Bella's tantrum last night, her insistence on having her father, Gabby should have realized how dangerous this was. If Bella saw them together or sensed the change in their relationship, she would make the natural assumption that Ryan—her dada—was here for good and make the times that he wasn't around even tougher.

The change was hard enough for Gabby to comprehend. She'd thought that moving to the ranch would make things easier, but now she wondered if she'd made an error. Too much change too fast, and to Bella's young mind, living on Ryan's property was the same as living with him.

If she and Ryan loved each other, it would be different. But he didn't love her. And she didn't—

The thought stopped her short, because she couldn't run from the truth any longer. She was falling for him.

Hard. All the more now that they'd slept together. The night had been even more incredible than that week they'd spent in Nashville. Gabby had let her guard down, and now her emotions were all over the place. Tender. Vulnerable. Exposed.

So of course her fears were multiplying at light speed. Especially since Ryan didn't reciprocate her feelings now any more than he had two and a half years ago.

Easing away from the warm strength of Ryan with more than a little regret, she tumbled out of bed and threw on an overlong T-shirt, needing to hold it together, but also needing to resurrect some boundaries. Fast.

"Ryan, you need to wake up," she said softly, frantically. She nudged his foot through the quilt, afraid if she moved any closer or touched his bare chest she would succumb to temptation. She still couldn't believe how easily she'd fallen back into his arms the night before. "You need to go home."

Rolling to his back, he blinked, sleepy confusion fogging his blue eyes. "Huh? What time is it?"

"Time for you to go. I don't want Bella to find you here." She picked up his jeans off the floor and tossed them onto the bed beside him. Where was his shirt? She turned away to search—and to avoid the sight of his lean body as he tugged on his pants.

"Gabby," he said, his voice a rumbly temptation. "Last night was—"

"A mistake," she said, cutting him off short. She passed him his boots and shirt. "I was a fool to think we could just resume our affair. It's not fair to Bella."

"Whoa, whoa, hold on a minute." He set aside the rest of his clothes and clasped her arms, his hands gentle as he stroked her skin. "Let's talk this through."

"Not now. Not when Bella could awaken and find us together at any time." She shook her head, stepping back even though she ached to lean into his embrace and draw in the scent of him. To lose herself in those sparks they'd rediscovered. "I've made up my mind. This can't happen again. It would be too confusing for Bella if things don't work out."

Her chest ached at the possibility that her actions could cause hurt for Bella down the road. She rubbed a hand absently along the phantom pain beneath her ribs.

"Why are you so insistent that this is destined to fail?" He hitched his hands on his hips, his muscular chest on full display. "Why not just continue as we have been, going on outings together, following the attraction wherever it leads?"

She swallowed hard, trying to keep her voice even. But it wasn't easy with him spouting off coolheaded advice when he wasn't the one suffering the pangs of deep emotions. But perhaps his detached reasoning was a welcome reminder that she couldn't afford a repeat of the night before. Not when he wasn't inclined to care for her beyond a co-parenting-with-benefits relationship.

That was not what she wanted.

"Because the longer we give Bella the impression that we're a couple, the more pain it will cause her if we split." And the more pain it would cause Gabby. She passed him his shirt and boots again, pushing them against his chest. "If we end this now, she won't think of us as together. She will think of us as her mama and dada, who have always lived in separate houses and slept in separate beds."

"Then marry me like I asked before," he said, his voice low, his eyes intense.

Because he was determined to get his way no matter the cost?

As much as she wanted to say yes, she couldn't. Not unless he was willing to give her his whole heart. "Are you asking since you've suddenly decided you love me after all?"

He stayed silent a heartbeat too long, turning to shrug into his flannel shirt and step into his boots.

The pain of that silence cut through her. She wouldn't be a fool over this man again. "Everything's too complicated between us. You say you don't want your child to have a contentious home life like the one you grew up in, but if we don't have love between us, then that's exactly what will happen."

His shoulders sagged with resignation. "You're set on this. No reservations?"

"For Bella, I am. Being a parent means making difficult choices. Do I have regrets? Of course. But do I have doubts? None. This is the right decision for Bella. Please, just go."

He stayed still for so long, she thought he would argue, and a tiny whisper inside her hoped that he would. That he might have the words, the love, that would convince her to let him stay.

But he simply shook his head, turned his back on her and walked out the door.

She held herself very still as she watched him leave, telling herself she would be okay. That she could recover from this defection even though she'd asked him for it. Yet the slow cracks widening all over her heart told her otherwise.

Her emotions in tatters, she did the only thing she could. She began packing.

Chapter Fourteen

Ryan had always prided himself on being logical. So having his tumultuous emotions push away rational thought threw him for a loop.

In the twelve hours since Gabby had tossed him out of her cabin, he hadn't been able to get her out of his mind. Not even when he'd rushed over to the barn, hearing about a cow that was having a difficult labor. The veterinarian had been called in.

Now, as he paced around the barn with his siblings waiting for news, he tried to busy himself with tasks...sorting tack, checking the levels in the automatic waterers, brushing Buzz. He would even sweep the floor if it took his mind off the searing ache of having Gabby boot him out of her bed, as well as her life.

Just when he'd convinced himself this might all blow over, she'd texted him that she was contacting her former landlord to see if another unit was available in the apartment complex since hers had been sublet, but that of course he could see Bella whenever he wished. He'd responded that he would like to bring Bella to see the new calf after it was born and they could speak more then. She'd answered that she would have Bella ready, but she wasn't prepared to discuss anything.

He was at a loss as to how to make headway with her.

Daniel drew up alongside him and clapped him on the shoulders. "What's going on? You look like someone took your last beer."

Seth and Allison glanced up from forking away damp bedding in a stall. He and his siblings knew the workings of the place from top to bottom, and didn't hesitate to roll up their sleeves on occasion. Unlike their father.

Ryan set aside the currycomb and leaned back against the stall. He might as well spill all. They would learn soon enough when Gabby relocated. "Gabby's moving out of the cabin. She said it's too confusing to Bella to have her thinking we live in the same place…" He winced, realizing he wasn't explaining it all. He'd held back out of pride. "We renewed our, uh, romance briefly. I asked her to marry me—so Bella wouldn't be confused—and Gabby turned me down."

Daniel hooked an arm around his shoulders and gave him a quick hug. "I'm sorry, man. That has to be tough."

Tough? Flat-out devastating. Like the world had dropped out from under his feet. Her reaction to their night together had caught him completely off guard. He'd fallen asleep happy beside her. Oblivious to the fears sleeping together had clearly stirred in her. He just didn't understand how a relationship could fall apart so fast.

So thoroughly that she was already working out a move.

Eloise cupped her hands around her infant in a front carrier, the baby's legs sticking out in a yellow foot sleeper. "As a new mom, I am sure that whatever Gabby decides, she is not making her decisions lightly. She came all the way to Bronco so that you could know your child. She didn't have to do that."

Charlotte was perched on a barrel petting a calico barn cat. "Technically, her job brought her here."

Eloise waved away her sister. "Ryan, don't listen to her. If Gabby was determined to keep you in the dark, she would not have accepted the transfer. She even agreed to move onto the ranch property just so Bella could be closer to you. So instead of guessing why she wants to leave, why don't you just talk to her?"

Seth stuck the pitchfork in the ground and leaned on the handle. "If you ask me, Ryan dodged a bullet. Women are more trouble than they're worth."

Allison snorted. "That sounds like something our father would say."

Seth splayed a hand over his heart. "Ouch, sorry. I wasn't serious." He pulled a wry grin. "I was just trying to lighten the mood."

Daniel angled closer, radiating that big-brother air he employed when doling out wisdom. "I'm wondering if you have feelings for Gabby that you haven't acknowledged. Like maybe you love her or this wouldn't be so gut-wrenching." He paused, letting those words sink in, then continued, "Have you really considered what Gabby would be up against if she became a part of our family?"

Ryan frowned, recalling how she'd lamented his parents' loveless marriage and wanting more for herself. And she'd been concerned about pressure Nora had put on her about not being from their social circle. Should he have discussed those issues with her in more detail? He speared a frustrated hand through his hair, hating that he didn't have an answer.

Charlotte smoothed a manicured hand over the cat's fur. "I agree. It can be hard to be a woman in Thaddeus Taylor's orbit. Maybe that's why Gabby wants to go."

Ryan's jaw clenched, his teeth grinding as he remembered the stunt their father pulled with intercepting Gabby's letters and messages. His stomach roiled all over again as he thought about Gabby alone and pregnant, trying to reach out to him. She'd handled the news so well that he hadn't dwelled on it overlong. But maybe that had been misguided. How would she have dealt with a father-in-law like that if Ryan ever managed to convince her to give him a chance?

Eloise smoothed a hand along his back much like she'd comforted her child. "Did any of that help?"

Help? He wasn't sure, but they'd given him a lot to think about. He scrubbed a hand over the back of his head just as all their cell phones buzzed with an incoming text, which saved him from responding to his sister's question.

Seth let out a whoop, waving his device in the air. "The cow delivered a healthy little bull calf."

Ryan reached for his jacket, relieved to have a new focus for his thoughts, if only briefly. "That's my cue to go get Bella so she can see the new baby. Thanks for the talk. I appreciate the support."

And he truly meant it. He hadn't spent as much time with his siblings in the past years as when they'd been growing up, but the bond was still there.

His parents may not have been able to come through for him, but he knew he could always count on his siblings. The sense of family he gained through them sustained him.

Or rather it had until now. Now he had a fierce need to grow his family so that it included Bella and Gabby, too.

Texting Gabby that he was on his way, he stepped

out into the chilly late-afternoon air, his gaze pinned on her cabin in the distance. He'd enjoyed having them both nearby. She'd said he could have unlimited access to Bella when they moved, but would she change her mind? Even if she stayed true to that vow, his contact with Gabby would be limited. And he hated the idea of not spending time with her. Of never holding her as he fell asleep again. Never waking up with her by his side. Already his heart felt empty, his life lonely in a way he'd never experienced before, not even in his father's worst rejections.

Because this was different. What he felt for Gabby could only be described as...

Love.

Enduring, to-the-depths-of-his-heart love.

How could he have been such a fool to miss it until now? He'd let his parents' marriage taint his view of commitment.

As he charged up the dirt path leading to her place, Ryan felt all the more certain of his feelings. And what he wanted for his future. Because he couldn't imagine being with anyone except Gabby. She and Bella were his family, his life. And while he didn't know exactly how to proceed next, he also wasn't giving up, no matter how long he had to wait.

His boots thudded up her porch steps and he knocked. Bella's squeal on the other side brought a much-needed smile. The door swung open—and Gabby looked as miserable as he'd felt. Beautiful, but utterly drained. She had dark circles under her eyes, and her face was pale. Elsie peeked around her leg, tail wagging.

Gabby stepped aside and waved him in, fidgeting with the neck of her company polo shirt. "I have some paperwork to complete. Bella's jacket and boots are on the sofa." She bent to give her daughter a kiss on the top of her head. "Have fun, sweetie, and be good for Dada. I love you."

The words made his gut clench for a split second before reason kicked in and he reminded himself that Gabby was addressing Bella. Seeing all the packing boxes and suitcases stacked in a corner didn't help, either.

He got the message loud and clear. She still wanted distance. To be fair, the realization of his love for her was still so new, he needed time to get his thoughts together before he had even a simple conversation with her. Gabby disappeared into the kitchen area, toward the nook with her computer desk. Once he turned around, Bella had already stepped into her boots and was running for the door with her coat.

"Hold on, kiddo," he called, jogging after her, just barely keeping Elsie from escaping. On the porch, he closed the door after them and eased Bella's jacket from her hand to help her put it on.

Bella blinked at him with wide eyes. "Mama come?"

"No," he said softly, tugging her zipper up, then

he clasped her hand to start back down the wooden stairs. "We need to let her work. She had a tough day. And when family love each other like we do, we help look out for each other. Do you understand? I love you, Bella."

"You wuv Mama, too?" Bella asked, hopping down each step.

"Yes, Bella," he answered without hesitation. "I love your mama very, very much."

Even though Bella likely didn't understand the full importance of what he'd said, Ryan had to admit that it felt good voicing his newly acknowledged feelings for Gabby. Swinging Bella up onto his shoulders, he just prayed that someday he would be able to say those same words to Gabby. But he needed to be sure the time was 100 percent right, because losing her due to a misstep was unthinkable.

Gabby hadn't managed to accomplish even one work task on her to-do list. Seeing Ryan today had brought a fresh wave of pain, along with regrets and second-guessing. How was she going to keep her distance from him week after week, year after year?

She'd tried to keep busy while he took Bella to see the calf, but mostly she'd only made a cup of coffee and paced around the cabin, Elsie watching her with wide and confused eyes.

"I feel the same, girl," Gabby said to her dog.

She'd never been so confused in her life, not even when she'd found herself pregnant and alone.

Two hours after Ryan and Bella had left, the thud of familiar boot steps climbing her porch steps echoed, followed by Bella's baby-babble. Nerves stirred the coffee around in her stomach. She grabbed a work file quickly and held it to her chest so it wouldn't be so obvious she'd wandered around aimlessly yearning for him the whole time they'd been gone.

She reached for the doorknob, bracing herself for the sight of him. And oh boy, did he look good. From his long legs encased in denim all the way to his wind-mussed blond hair.

Gulping, she said, "Hello, Ryan."

He simply nodded before kneeling to give Bella a hug goodbye. He bolted back down the stairs so quickly it made her eyes sting with tears and hurt all over again. What in the world was he running from now?

Shouldn't she be glad he hadn't pressed her? She'd told him this was what she wanted. She pushed aside the thoughts to mull over later. For now, she needed to get through Bella's evening routine.

Heaven help her if her child asked for a night-night kiss from Dada again.

Drawing in a shaky breath, Gabby forced a smile on her face for her daughter as she closed the door behind Ryan after his hasty departure. "Did you have a good time seeing the new baby calf?"

"Baby cow." She demonstrated what Gabby assumed was a baby calf walk with a wide-legged stagger, her pigtails swishing as she giggled.

Seeing her daughter so happy poured guilt on top of Gabby's wounded heart. She was trying to do her best for Bella, but providing emotional stability was so much tougher than anyone could have imagined.

Hopelessness—helplessness—blindsided her and a lone tear rolled down her cheek. Gabby dropped to sit on the sofa, scrubbing her wrist across her face. Her hand trembled. She needed to get herself together before she upset her daughter.

Bella scrambled up onto the couch and tucked herself right up against Gabby's side, Elsie pouncing to claim the other. Tears burned hotter.

Her daughter rested her head against Gabby's shoulder, patting her arm. "Wuv you, Mama. Dada wuvs you."

Gabby went still inside. Then the tears spilled over and down. Bella couldn't possibly know what she'd said.

"Thank you, sweetie." Gabby slipped an arm around her daughter. "Dada loves you very much. You're his special little girl."

Bella hitched up onto her knees and put her chubby hands on either side of Gabby's face just as Gabby did to Bella when she needed the child's full attention. "Dada wuvs you. Dada wuvs you."

Wait, what? Surely Bella must have misunderstood,

except the toddler was so emphatic, so sure as she repeated the words again and again. And no question, she was at an age where she parroted whatever she heard.

But if Ryan felt this way, why wouldn't he tell her? That just didn't make sense. Why would he insist he wanted nothing more from her than sex and a loveless marriage? Because if he loved her, that was a game changer.

And if he didn't? Then he needed to guard his words better around Bella, because it wasn't fair to mislead the child and give her hope that they would ever live under the same roof.

One thing she did know for certain. The moment Bella fell asleep, Gabby would be confronting Ryan with what Bella said.

Ryan made it as far as halfway home before he stopped in his tracks, hanging his head.

Yes, his siblings' words from earlier had made him realize he'd been doing a lot of assuming and not much real communicating with Gabby. But waiting for the perfect time to talk was only a stall tactic to further protect his heart. He'd allowed her to push him away without being honest about his feelings for her.

No more stalling.

Sure, even if he confessed his love for her, she still might not want him, but she deserved to know that he loved her. He hadn't come through for her two and half years ago by calling after their affair and that was a mistake he would regret for the rest of his life.

He wasn't going to make the same mistake again.

Pivoting, he started the walk back, picking up speed and jogging the rest of the way, sidestepping a pothole and ducking under a low branch. He made it to her fence just as Gabby stepped out into the yard to let Elsie run. Bella followed and sat on the top step, her elbows on her knees, her chin in her hands.

He muttered a silent prayer of thanks that Bella somehow understood the need to stay still for just a moment.

"Ryan?" Gabby gasped, her brown eyes wary.

With joy or hesitation?

Either way, the next step was his.

"Gabby," he said as he swept open the gate, "is there a chance we can talk tonight?"

Slowly, she nodded. "Okay, but when you're finished it's my turn."

"Whatever you need to say." Good or bad, he could take it, as long as he was honest with her now. "If after you hear what I need to say, you still want to move, I'll respect the decision and I won't pressure you."

"I'm listening," she said softly, chewing her bottom lip.

He clasped her hands in his. He'd once thought that the mountains of Montana were the most beautiful sight on earth. He now knew he was wrong. This incredible woman won, hands down. "Gabby, I understand that you may not feel the same way, but I need for you to know that I am madly, deeply in love with you. I've probably been in love with you all along, but I've just been too much of a lunkhead to believe I could be this lucky."

The words that had once seemed so impossible to say now tumbled from him with ease.

Bella called out to him from the top step. "I wuv you, too, Dada."

Her baby sweetness nearly broke him. Looking down into eyes so like his own, the miracle of family twining around him, the real sense of a forever family hit home for him.

Looking over his shoulder, he extended a hand to his daughter and she raced full speed to clasp his in hers. "I love you as well, Bella. I'm the luckiest dad in the world to have a little girl like you."

He owed so much of his happiness to her mother for bringing Bella into his life. His gaze turned to Gabby.

She'd stayed so silent. Was she about to reject him the same way she'd done after they'd made love? Would she be upset that he'd said he loved her in front of Bella? He hadn't thought about that, had only been focused on making sure Gabby knew how he felt. But what was she thinking? Swallowing down the lump of emotion—and fear—clogging his throat, he finally looked back at Gabby.

Tears streamed unchecked down her face. Were they happy tears or…?

"Ryan…" Her hand trembled as she raised it to her mouth. "I'm scared. Scared of loving, scared of losing, scared that your feelings might change."

Nodding, he hated that he'd made her feel this way. He tapped himself on the chest right over his heart. "I understand that. Truly I do. I know that love can be scary. But I'm more afraid of spending another day without you in my life."

He had so much more that he needed to say to Gabby, but he didn't want Bella to overhear if they had trouble to iron out.

He knelt in front of his daughter. "Why don't you go play on your swing while I talk to your mama for a minute?"

"Yes, Dada…" Bella took off running to her tire swing and tucked her body through, swaying. Elsie ran in a circle, chasing her tail.

Ryan turned back to Gabby and didn't let another moment pass. "Gabby, my love, I realized something today that should have been so obvious from the start. My reservations about commitment were based on faulty logic—because I am not my father. And on the subject of my dad, I will be speaking to him. I will make sure he understands the boundary around my family and that I won't tolerate him ever overstepping on my watch."

"Thank you—for Bella's sake in particular, thank you."

He took her hands in his and pressed them over his thudding heart. "I know what true love is now, thanks to you. If you'll have me, I would like us to be married, a real marriage. I'll wait, if that's what you need, but know that I intend to prove my love for you every single day for the rest of our lives."

More tears leaked from her eyes, but her smile made it clear they were happy ones. She threw her arms around his neck, whispering against his mouth, "Of course I love you, too. You fill my heart and my life. I can't wait to see what the future has in store for us."

With a whoop, he swung her around, then lowered her to seal their vow with a kiss. "And what an incredible future it promises to be."

As her feet touched the ground, she looped her arms around his neck. "What do you say we feed our daughter supper and read her bedtime stories together. Then, we can continue this conversation, just the two of us."

"Yes, ma'am," he said with a wink. "There's nothing I would like more."

Epilogue

Two weeks later

The sun was sinking behind a mountain on the most wonderful day of Gabby's life. She was done moving. This marked her final relocation. Today, she and Bella were moving in with Ryan, officially beginning their life together as a family.

From Ryan's front yard, she directed the last of the packers unloading the truck full of furniture from storage. Others carried the final boxes from the cabin. The past two weeks, she and Ryan had spent every possible moment—day and night—together, until over their dinner last weekend, Ryan had asked her to move in with him.

Her answer had been easy. Immediate.

Waving the movers into the house, she strode up the wide steps leading to the front porch of Ryan's log home. Their home now. The sun shone high above in the unpolluted sky, the winds sweeping around the mountains carrying the sweet scent of spring, of new life.

Just like her new beginning with Ryan, blooming with promise.

She should have been exhausted from the rapid move, but the outpouring of help had been incredible. Ryan's siblings had been so welcoming, rolling up their sleeves to smooth the transition. Imogen had taken Bella for a tea party picnic under a fat oak tree to keep her occupied.

Her dear friend Rylee had come by on her lunch break with a housewarming basket of goodies. And others from the town had stopped in as well, so many she would need a second notebook to keep track of all they'd done for her. They'd brought fresh canned goods, homemade soaps, a welcome mat, beeswax scented candles, fresh-baked dog treats for Elsie. The list went on and on.

And most of all, Ryan had gone above and beyond to make her feel cherished since he'd obviously been planning this ever since he'd confessed to his feelings for her. He'd outfitted an incredible home office for her, a beautiful retreat for when she needed to work remotely. The details had been so thorough and thoughtful she suspected his sisters had assisted.

Which touched her all the more. He'd even included a puzzle table, with special drawers for piece sorting.

As for Bella, he'd asked for Gabby's help in creating the perfect nursery for their daughter. Her current room was lovely, but in a few weeks' time, Bella would have a place that was all the more personal, reflecting her special interests. And, of course, reflecting a father's love for his little girl. Gabby could have never anticipated the care and thought Ryan would put into making sure Bella knew she was loved. He'd even started working on an agility course area for Elsie and said he looked forward to training the pup.

Familiar boot steps echoed from indoors, then onto the porch. Her heart raced and a smile filled her heart. Every day with Ryan was better than the last.

Ryan slung his arm around her shoulders. "I had them put the last of the boxes in one of the spare bedrooms so they would be out of the way until we're ready to decide where to put the rest. Is everything where you want it? Because if it isn't, just let me know."

She'd integrated some of the furniture from her home into the decor, and other pieces were going into a new vacation cabin under construction in the mountains nearby. They'd found the perfect blend for their lives.

She leaned against his side, and his hard muscled chest stirred her. "Today has gone smoother than I could have imagined thanks to all the help. I can't believe how many people stopped by. Did you hear Winona and Stanley's news when they brought cookies?"

"No, I must have missed seeing them."

"Well," she said, excited to be one of the first to know, "Winona finally set a date. Drumroll… They're getting married in July. Winona said she would have been content with a justice of the peace, but Stanley wanted a white wedding."

"That's fantastic," he said, a dimple denting his cheek. "No doubt, it will be an event to remember with all of Bronco in attendance. You're a part of our community now, you know."

"Everyone's support today means the world to me." For someone who moved so often and had no living family members other than her child—and now Ryan—being welcomed into the Bronco circle brought tears to her eyes. "And Bella is loving being spoiled by her grandma. I snapped some amazing photos of your mom and Bella's tea party. Maybe we can frame one for Imogen."

"Thank you for making the effort with my mom. She hasn't had an easy life." His forehead furrowed with worry and stress.

Thaddeus had made a brief appearance. He'd apologized and brought her an over-the-top fresh flower arrangement. He'd even brought a children's book about cowgirls for Bella and presented it in his typical stuffy manner. While Gabby knew it was unlikely he'd experienced a significant change of heart so quickly, at least he was going through the motions. It was a start. She understood that any family came with their own set of rewards and challenges. She was very ready to find joy in the former while navigating the latter. In fact, she couldn't wait.

Gabby caressed her fingers over his furrowed forehead until it smoothed. "I hope you know how much I love you."

"If you love me even half as much as I love you, then there's nothing we can't handle. You and I are a team. Now and forever." He winked playfully. "I even cleared out a closet for you in my bedroom— and a space for you in my heart."

She rested her head on his shoulder. "We've sure overcome the odds to make our very own happily-ever-after."

He tucked a knuckle under her chin and tipped her face up to his. "What do you say we make it official?"

Everything inside her went still. Was he actually proposing? She didn't want to assume. "What do you mean?"

Smoothly, he dropped to one knee, the backdrop of his home the perfect setting for this moment. He pulled out a small, black velvet box from his jeans pocket and opened the lid.

A stunning diamond engagement ring glittered in the sunlight. Her hands flew to her mouth in surprise and happiness.

"Gabby, I know it may be too soon, but this is

where I see us heading. I hope that someday you will be ready to put it on. I'm willing to wait for however long it takes."

She let herself savor this beautiful moment of all her dreams coming true, then extended her left hand. "How about now?"

He exhaled in such obvious relief it touched her as much as the proposal itself.

Ryan slid the ring on her finger, a perfect fit, and sealed its placement with a kiss. Standing, he folded her hand against his heart. "I never thought I'd find the right person for me."

"It's never too late to fall in love." Thank goodness they'd found their way back to each other. "Just look at Winona and Stanley."

"Maybe we could have a double ceremony," he said jokingly.

"Not a chance, cowboy." She arched up, her lips against his. "I want you all for myself."

"Yes, ma'am," he said as he kissed her once, twice.

Her toes curled in her boots with pleasure—and anticipation for taking the kiss further. But first… "What do you say we tell Bella the good news?"

He clasped her hand, squeezing gently, his blue eyes full of love. "Lead the way, beautiful, because I'm never losing you again. Wherever you go, I'm happy to follow."

* * * * *

Look for the next installment in the new continuity
Montana Mavericks: The Anniversary Gift

The Maverick's Marriage Deal
by Kaylie Newell

On sale April 2024
wherever Harlequin books and ebooks are sold.

And don't miss

Sweet-Talkin' Maverick
by Christy Jeffries

Available now!

COMING NEXT MONTH FROM

⚡HARLEQUIN
SPECIAL EDITION

#3039 TAKING THE LONG WAY HOME
Bravo Family Ties • by Christine Rimmer
After one perfect night with younger rancher Jason Bravo, widowed librarian Piper Wallace is pregnant with his child. Co-parenting is a given. But Jason will do anything—even accompany her on a road trip to meet her newly discovered biological father—to prove he's playing for keeps!

#3040 SNOWED IN WITH A STRANGER
Match Made in Haven • by Brenda Harlen
Party planner Finley Gilmore loves an adventure, but being snowbound with Professor Lachlan Kellett takes *tempted by a handsome stranger* to a whole new level! Their chemistry could melt a glacier. But when Lachlan's past resurfaces, will Finlay be the one iced out?

#3041 A FATHER'S REDEMPTION
The Tuttle Sisters of Coho Cove • by Sabrina York
Working with developer Ben Sherrod should have turned Celeste Tuttle's dream project into a nightmare. Except the single father is witty and brilliant and so much more attractive than she remembered from high school. Could her childhood nemesis be Prince Charming in disguise?

#3042 MATZAH BALL BLUES
Holidays, Heart and Chutzpah • by Jennifer Wilck
Entertainment attorney Jared Leiman will do anything to be the guardian his orphaned niece needs. Even reunite with Caroline Weiss, his high school ex, to organize his hometown's Passover ball with the Jewish Community Center. Sparks fly...but he'll need a little matzah magic to win her over.

Get 3 FREE REWARDS!

We'll send you 2 FREE Books plus a FREE Mystery Gift.

FREE
Value Over
$20

Both the **Harlequin® Special Edition** and **Harlequin® Heartwarming™** series feature compelling novels filled with stories of love and strength where the bonds of friendship, family and community unite.

YES! Please send me 2 FREE novels from the Harlequin Special Edition or Harlequin Heartwarming series and my FREE Gift (gift is worth about $10 retail). After receiving them, if I don't wish to receive any more books, I can return the shipping statement marked "cancel." If I don't cancel, I will receive 6 brand-new Harlequin Special Edition books every month and be billed just $5.49 each in the U.S. or $6.24 each in Canada, a savings of at least 12% off the cover price, or 4 brand-new Harlequin Heartwarming Larger-Print books every month and be billed just $6.24 each in the U.S. or $6.74 each in Canada, a savings of at least 19% off the cover price. It's quite a bargain! Shipping and handling is just 50¢ per book in the U.S. and $1.25 per book in Canada.* I understand that accepting the 2 free books and gift places me under no obligation to buy anything. I can always return a shipment and cancel at any time by calling the number below. The free books and gift are mine to keep no matter what I decide.

Choose one: ☐ **Harlequin Special Edition** (235/335 BPA GRMK)   ☐ **Harlequin Heartwarming Larger-Print** (161/361 BPA GRMK)   ☐ **Or Try Both!** (235/335 & 161/361 BPA GRPZ)

Name (please print)

Address   Apt. #

City   State/Province   Zip/Postal Code

Email: Please check this box ☐ if you would like to receive newsletters and promotional emails from Harlequin Enterprises ULC and its affiliates. You can unsubscribe anytime.

Mail to the **Harlequin Reader Service:**
IN U.S.A.: P.O. Box 1341, Buffalo, NY 14240-8531
IN CANADA: P.O. Box 603, Fort Erie, Ontario L2A 5X3

Want to try 2 free books from another series! Call 1-800-873-8635 or visit www.ReaderService.com.

---

*Terms and prices subject to change without notice. Prices do not include sales taxes, which will be charged (if applicable) based on your state or country of residence. Canadian residents will be charged applicable taxes. Offer not valid in Quebec. This offer is limited to one order per household. Books received may not be as shown. Not valid for current subscribers to the Harlequin Special Edition or Harlequin Heartwarming series. All orders subject to approval. Credit or debit balances in a customer's account(s) may be offset by any other outstanding balance owed by or to the customer. Please allow 4 to 6 weeks for delivery. Offer available while quantities last.

HSEHW23